Copyright (

Paperback]
Hardcover]
Imprint: Independently Published
All Rights Reserved
Printed in the USA
Cover by A. A. Medina (Fabled Beast Design)
This book is a work of fiction. Any similarity to persons or events in reality is totally inconsequential and unintended.
No part of this written work may be reprinted without the author's permission.
An Occasional Portal, INNARDS-FUCK, and *Anti-VaXXX* were originally included in the collection *Your God Can't Save You* (publication date April 25, 2022). The versions of these stories in this book have been edited and expanded upon. The rest of the stories in this collection are being published here for the very first time.

Trigger Warning:
This is an extreme horror collection. If you do not like to read uncomfortable books, then you will not enjoy reading this one.

TOXIC

Other Books by Judith Sonnet
We Have Summoned
Cabin Possessions
For the Sake Of
For the Sake Of (2)
Torture the Sinners!
The Clown Hunt
Greta's Fruitcup
Chainsaw Hooker
Something Akin to Revulsion
Low Blasphemy
No One Rides for Free
Magick
Kill Yer Pumpkins
Jump Scare
Blood Suck
Gobbler: Fuck Your Thanksgiving
Earth Vs. The Nudist Camp Freaks
Zombie Vomit Shitshow
Santasploitation
Repugnant (The Goddamned Edition)
Summer Never Ends
Sardines (In the Dark)
Carnage on 84th Street: Splatter Crimes
Fetid Festivities

TOXIC

TOXIC

A Collection
By
Judith Sonnet

TOXIC

TOXIC

Table of Contents:

An Occasional Portal... 9

INNARDS-FUCK... 32

What Are You Going to Do with Me? ... 48

Toxic... 77

The Cum House... 112

Anti-VaXXX... 143

Wee-Gee... 155

Sally... 194

Cruising for Creeps... 202

Afterword... 243

TOXIC

For
Duncan Ralston
For the support, the laughs, and the gross-outs

TOXIC

TOXIC

An Occasional Portal

It was a chilly night in February the first time Stew Ripley noticed the revolving door.

He was, admittedly, a little drunk. His bladder was pinching his belly, and his head felt hollow. Even his bones seemed to ripple with inebriation.

Stew was walking alongside a close friend when he spied the door.

It was across the street. Unassuming except for its ornate lintel. The top of the door was crusted with age, but Stew could see a line of intricate faces beaming down toward him.

Three faces in all.

The middle one was hairy and stern, with squinting eyes and almond shaped teeth. The faces to either side of the angry man were identical to each other. They were womanly, with long hair that flowed toward the man, and congregated behind him.

The glass on the door was opaque. It looked as if the revolving door hadn't been attended to in years.

The building itself was also inconspicuous. A flat, gray, and bland two-story storefront, crammed in between an apartment complex and a warehouse.

TOXIC

"What's that?" Stew slurred and pointed toward the building.

Layton peered across the street slowly, as if he needed glasses. "I don't know. Probably used to be a retail outlet or something."

"How come," he belched, "how come no one's done anything with it?" Stew asked.

"Bad location." Layton shrugged. "What the hell am I supposed to know about it, Stewart?"

Stew realized that he was being drawn toward the revolving door. He wanted to push his way into one of its glass quarters and allow it to sweep him into the vacant building.

But what would he find inside?

Surely nothing more interesting than a party of abandoned mannequins and maybe some collapsed ceiling tiles.

Stew pushed away his odd desire to be near the revolving door, hiccupped, and hailed a passing taxi.

On the ride home, Layton and Stewart spoke briefly about other matters.

"Are you going to see her again?" Layton asked, referring to a colleague Stew had taken on a date.

She was young, and modest, with long red hair and smart glasses. She looked, to Stew, like the complete opposite of his blonde and round ex-wife.

He had realized, on their date, that this detail had been the only thing that had attracted him toward Felicia. It was the simple fact that she wasn't at all like his ex. He didn't care about her opinions, her stories, or even her body.

And now, unfortunately, he had to either continue dating her to save face at work or break up with her and see if she quit.

He might have to find an excuse to fire her.

He wished that Layton hadn't brought the matter up.

Stewart Ripley knew he was a piece of shit... and that his behavior was deplorable. And yet he found himself doing bad things without hesitation.

He and Annie had gotten a divorce only because she had walked in on him laying one of her best friends. The whole seduction and affair had been no more than a sport for Stew.

And he hadn't felt bad about it even while Annie screamed at him and demanded that he leave.

In fact, he had turned over and watched as Annie's bestie hurriedly dressed and wept her way out of the room.

He had been curious about her response.

Some people chose to fight, while others chose to fly.

Annie's pal was a flyer.

"I don't know." Stew shifted in his seat and burped. He hoped he wasn't on the verge of vomiting. Something acrid was scuttling up his throat.

"Well, you're going to see her tomorrow at least, right? I mean, she is my secretary. I'd feel like shit if she asks me about you every day."

"Yeah. I'll see her tomorrow. But I made it clear to her... work is work. She's not going to try anything funny there."

"You can't pretend to separate business from pleasure if you're mixing them after hours." Layton frowned.

"Don't preach at me." Stew looked out the window, knowing he could bring up Layton's own proclivities as well. "Anyways... where are we going?"

"I thought we were going home?" Layton ran a hand through his long, blonde hair.

"Nah. The night is young. And I could use the headache as an excuse tomorrow."

"An excuse to not talk to Felicia?"

"That and whatever else may come up."

"Driver?" Layton leaned forward. "Let's change destinations. How about *Spunky's*?"

Stew lifted his arm and took in a breath. He smelled like sweat and booze. His body felt sticky, and he could feel the hairs along his belly crawling awkwardly against his shirt.

Stew was a large man, with a thick carpet of chest hair that peered out beneath his silver beard. His eyes were black and narrow, hidden behind a pair of horn-rimmed glasses. His fingers were porky, and he still wore his golden wedding band. He claimed, to friends, that he had trouble pulling the damn thing off. To lovers, he either said that he was still married, or that poor Annie had passed away; whichever added more of a thrill to their escapade.

When the taxicab turned around, Stew made sure to watch the street as it rolled by. He saw many things that caught his eye. Suits in store fronts, lines outside night clubs, even a man urinating in an alley way—which gave him a chuckle.

But the thing that stood out, to his surprise, was the revolving door at the vacant lot. As the taxi drove by it, he felt as if time was slowed. For just a moment, he could see the door with sober clarity.

It was turning.

Someone was in it... pushing through.

They were barely visible in the haze of dust that clouded the glass, but he could tell that the figure was female. She had long gray hair and was wearing a purple dress.

He was surprised that the door was unlocked and that just *anybody* could walk into a potentially dangerous and unused space. He wondered if the building housed homeless people, or drug addicts.

What if she's the owner?

Or maybe... she's planning on buying the lot and making something out of it.

Could make an alright nightclub.

Nah. It's on the wrong side of town. No one rich would come out here... unless they're soused, like me and Layton.

As his mind wandered, his eyes fuzzed over. In the haze, he saw something impossible.

The woman pushing through the door vanished.

She didn't come out the other side only to disintegrate into the shadows.

No.

She merely *dissipated* before the door had made a complete rotation. In fact, the door stopped, which should have sealed her in the netherworld space between the wall and the lot.

She was simply and inexplicably gone. A ghost that had lost its image.

Stew craned his neck to watch the door as they drove past it. He expected his vision to reacclimatize to the darkness and to the blurs of motion... but they didn't.

The woman, whoever she was, was simply gone.

And so too—eventually—was the door.

"Stewart?" Layton drew Stew away from the revolving door.

"Huh?" Stew asked dumbly.

"Have you heard a single word I've said?"

The next day, Stew woke up with a headache. It was a dull and thumping pain that drew its talons across his brain.

It pissed acid through his nerves.

He rolled out of bed and looked down at his swollen gut. He felt like absolute and total shit. He also felt like he deserved it all. With hangovers came guilt, and with guilt came an unnecessary backtracking through his history of poor judgment and toxic behaviors.

Stew stood in the shower and tried to focus on happier thoughts. He tried to remember what had happened last night at *Spunky's*...

...but all that stood out to him was the revolving door. With its three overseers, and its dusty glass.

His fixation made no sense.

Then, he remembered the woman... walking through the door and not coming out at the other end.

Stew got out of the shower, rubbed his balding head with a towel.

He walked into his kitchen naked. Stew left wet footprints on the tile floor. Opening the fridge, Stew stared blankly into it. He had orange juice, a packet of hotdogs, and a bag of grapes. None of them appealed to his hangover.

Stew straightened up and pinched his eyes closed. He'd have to waddle out of his apartment for breakfast, it seemed. He really didn't want to go through the hassle of it all, but his belly was groaning, and he needed a plate of hash browns and an exaggerated helping of hot sauce.

When he turned around, he was only dimly surprised to see Layton lying on his coach. His buddy had apparently been too drunk to go to his own apartment.

Stew was thankful Layton was still asleep. It gave him time to rush back to his room and throw on a pair of pants and tuck in a plain tee. When he came back to the living room, Layton was groggily sitting up and rubbing his crusty eyes.

"What time is it?" Layton asked.

"Early." Stew looked toward the clock on his oven. "I've got about two hours before I have to be at the office."

Layton yawned and threw his arms over his head. "I feel like an elephant sat on my head."

"Want breakfast?" Stew offered.

"What do you have?"

"I was thinking *Mike's*." Stew referred to the diner two blocks over.

Layton took a shower and brushed his teeth—using his finger—before the two men set out for breakfast.

They talked dully on their way through the elevator and out the lobby.

As the automatic door slid open for them, Stew once again found his mind wandering back to the vacant lot. It really refused to leave his head. It was like a tick, embedded under his skin. Even if he plucked it out, he was certain that a part of it would detach and sink into his body.

"Remember the revolving door?" Stew found himself asking.

"No. What? Is that another club? I thought we finished things off at S*punky's*."

"No. A real door. A revolving one. The one that led into that vacant building... we saw it last night."

"Oh. Barely." Layton had not been cursed with Stew's peculiar fascination.

"I thought I saw someone go through it." Stew stated.

"Yeah?"

Stew realized that Layton had expected more.

He wasn't sure what he had even hoped to accomplish by bringing the door up.

Maybe he had just wanted to test it out and see if it was real.

All Layton could confirm was that the door had indeed existed.

Stew felt like a fool. His face grew appropriately red.

"Yeah." Stew concluded and pulled his arms around his chest.

It was starting to snow.

The door didn't leave his mind.

At work, he saw it every time he closed his eyes.

When Felecia came into his office during her lunch break and tried to ask him if they could schedule another date, Stew almost interrupted her to ask her if she had ever seen the revolving door on Lewis Avenue.

He had to stop himself by agreeing to a date on Tuesday, after work.

He even promised to take her somewhere fancy, which was just cruel.

Her eyes lit up and she couldn't contain a blush. Stew felt his heart sink into his stomach.

On his own lunch break—while he ate Chinese takeout—he wondered if he shouldn't visit the door. It was clear that it had no intention of leaving his psyche. He looked down at his plate of orange chicken and found his appetite had become curdled.

What an innocuous and bizarre thing to have formed a fixation on!

Stew couldn't remember a single revolving door in his life without exerting his brain. Yet he was recalling the most miniscule details of this particular door.

As if he had developed a photographic memory.

TOXIC

He saw the three faces—a leering and hairy man between two smooth and vacant women. Their flowing hair was speckled with rust and damage.

The store's front was dark and empty. Its windows were so dusty, they looked like nylon.

The lot itself was almost cowering beneath the buildings at its sides.

And Stew realized he wanted to go to it.

He wanted to investigate the door... to push it forward and watch it rotate.

It was truly the door itself and not the building it led into that charmed him so.

He couldn't help it. All he could think about was a revolving door. Of all things he could waste his time and energy on... he was focused on a revolving door.

He waited for work to end like a student watching the clock on the last day of school. When he was finished, he dashed past Felicia—who was chatting with his secretary—and raced toward the elevator. When he reached the street, he realized he had left his jacket in his office. Instead of retrieving it, he barreled forward. He wasn't able to turn around.

He had to be on Lewis Avenue.

He had to see the door.

The cab ride was an endurance test. His nerves jumped beneath his skin and his stomach did somersaults. When he stepped out of the cab and found himself standing at the revolving door, Stew felt his heart crawl up his throat and rest in his mouth.

TOXIC

The revolving door was just as mystifying in person as it had become in his head. With its ornate lintel, its tile floor, and its dirty glass. It was ugly and gorgeous all at once.

He reached forward and touched one of the glass panels. He fully expected it to electrocute him. There was a warm energy that coursed out of the door... as if the building it was affixed to was filled with hot air conditioners.

Stew stared up at the middle face on the lintel. The man's expression returned his stare with a hard scowl. Up close, Stew saw that whoever had crafted the beam had paid close attention to the middle face. He had a cleft lip, and his sharpened teeth barley contained a prodding tongue.

Sharpened teeth? Stew thought. *This guy could bite a shark back!*

Stew pulled his hand back and stepped away from the door.

He peered through the murky storefront.

He could barely see into the lot, but he could tell that it had been gutted. The ceiling was open, exposing light fixtures, tangled wires, and ripped tubes. The floor was powdered with broken ceiling tiles, junk food wrappers, and there was even an upturned trashcan in the very center of the lot. It reaffirmed his theory that the lot itself wasn't at all fascinating or interesting.

It was the door...

Stew sighed and stepped back, crossing his arms over his chest. His teeth chattered as a cold burst of wind hit him.

Behind him, cars rushed by.

A woman walked past, talking on her phone.

A row of pigeons fluttered off of the roof of the vacant building.

The whole world moved around Stew as if nothing had changed... and yet it all felt distant.

Unobtainable.

He could never return to the real world, or interact with it, until he had completed his task.

All he had to do was push the door forward and walk in. He'd be trapped for a brief moment between two glass panels and a curved wall.

And then he'd be in the building...

But why? Why had this become so important to him?

He had almost entirely forgotten about the woman that had walked through the door last night. The door had stopped moving, and she had ceased to be.

What had become of her?

He had to know.

He had to...

He was already inside the door. His hands rested on the supportive bar ahead of him and pushed the panels forward like a shopping cart. He strained his eyes as the warmth of the building swaddled him.

The door caught on the floor and came to a jarring halt.

Stew opened his eyes.

He was stuck where the woman had vanished... in the space between street and property.

TOXIC

Ahead of him, he saw the interior of the building more clearly. There was nothing appealing or welcoming about the building's insides. It looked threatening, even. Like what he imagined a crack-den or a crime scene to look like. He even saw, now, that there was a dead rat lying on its back amid the spilled trash.

It wasn't the building that was so cordial and warm. It was just *this* space. This tiny area, sectioned off from the world.

He could stand comfortably in here for hours.

Stew felt as if all of his worries were leaking out of his body and pooling beneath him.

Stew realized that he wasn't at all panicked, even though he couldn't seem to progress any further. The door was stuck, and it refused to budge. This was where Stew existed now. Crammed in against a curved wall, his nose itching with dust, and his breath coming out in hot gasps.

He should have been uncomfortable, but he might as well have been hugged by his mother.

Stew turned his head—

—and his breath was immediately arrested.

The curved wall had been replaced. Instead, he was looking down a long and dark hallway.

The hallway was narrow and slicked with dripping water, as if Stew had been transported into the middle of a sewer. Green patches of moss and fungus grew on the ceiling, hanging down in moist clumps.

TOXIC

A cold breath wheezed out from the end of the tunnel and beat against Stew's face. His sweat froze against his skin.

This can't be real. This has to be a dream...

A nightmare.

There was something at the end of the tunnel. A malformed figure. It limped forward, its hands braced against the tunnel walls for support. Its head tilted forward and to the side, as if its neck could barely support it.

Stew gripped the railing ahead of him and began to jostle it. He no longer wanted to be here. He wanted to get away from the cool tunnel and from its occupant.

He cursed his curiosity and his fixation.

All he wanted to do was move forward.

He looked down the tunnel and watched as the figure approached on rickety legs. The closer it grew the more details he noticed.

It was the woman.

He couldn't possibly know her name, and he hadn't even seen her face... and yet he knew it was her.

She was round and had long brown hair, which hung in tangled knots down her shoulders. She was naked and her skin was sallow. It looked like wet paper hung out on a clothesline. He flesh was simply draped over her bones, as if all her insides had been sucked out. She looked deflated. *Yes, that was the word: deflated.*

She bore injuries that should have been fatal and yet she still walked.

TOXIC

A large chunk was missing from the right side of her throat, exposing the white pipe of her esophagus. Delicate red strands hung out of the wound, pumping black and yellow fluids.

Blood quilted her legs and hands, as if she was wearing red gloves.

Her fingernails were long and curved, and she was missing her thumbs.

Stew wondered if he should scream. If he should beat his fists against the glass and see if they broke. He wondered if a passerby would notice him, or if he had simply vanished from sight... as this ghoulish woman had only twenty hours ago.

She was getting closer. A low growl issued from her broken throat. She tilted her head upward, exposing her face. Her lips were peeled away from her teeth. Her tongue had been destroyed. It had been chewed so violently it looked like the end of a used cigar.

Stew turned around and pushed toward the street. The door inched backward, moving with some resistance but not fast enough. The woman was almost upon him now... reaching out with twisted fingers.

Her eyes were blind. They were as white as saucers, and they leaked red tears.

"Oh, God!" Stew called out. "Oh, God!"

The woman uttered a garbled word. One that both surprised Stew and drew currents of fear through his body.

She said: "Help..."

The door finally gave in, and Stew spilled out onto the street.

He collided with a passing woman, who yelped and leapt aside. He hit the pavement, jarring his head against the ground and knocking his teeth together. He was aware that he was bleeding out of his lower lip. He began to scuttle forward and toward the street.

He was shouting: "Please! Let me go! Please!"

"Whoa! Whoa!"

Two strong hands grasped him by the shoulders and yanked him back. He—at first—thought that the hideous ghoul had caught up to him... until his senses came to him. A Good Samaritan was holding him back from crawling into traffic.

"Hold on, mister... you're gonna kill yourself!" The man sounded as if he was scolding a child instead of a full grown and weighty man.

Stew collapsed into tears. He gripped the hands of the man and began to cry up toward his face: "Oh, thank God! Thank, God!"

He didn't know how to explain everything that had just happened to him, or if it was even worth trying. He looked crazy enough; he didn't want to push it any further.

"Listen, dude... do you want me to call you an ambulance or something?"

"No! No!" Stew shook his head.

The life-saver was bearded and wore a knit skull-cap. His face was worried, and his hands were strong.

TOXIC

The woman Stew had stumbled into was standing by the revolving doors, looking disheveled and concerned.

A small crowd was growing around them.

"I-" Stew looked for an explanation. "I was-"

"What happened?" An onlooker asked.

"I was-" Stew stumbled through his words. "I... I was almost mugged... in the alley. I was taking a shortcut and a guy jumped out with a knife."

"I thought you-" The woman pointed toward the doors.

"Yes, I ran away from him and hid in that building and got caught in the doors. I'm afraid— I'm afraid I had a panic attack." Stew coughed into his fist and began to smooth his front down, as if he was recovering from a tumble.

"Where is he?" The bearded man asked.

"Who?"

"The goddamn mugger?" The bearded man's patience was waning.

"Oh. I-I don't know." Stew felt his face grow red. "I think he ran off."

"Well, we should call the police." The bearded man and a stringy teen helped Stew up to his feet.

Stew shook their hands afterwards and said: "I don't see why. He didn't take anything. I didn't even get a proper look at him."

"Well, Jesus Christ... be careful, dude." The bearded man shook his head and walked off.

The crowd had already lost interest in Stew. They began to dissolve around him. Even the disheveled woman was nowhere to be seen.

Soon it was Stew and Stew alone... standing by the vacant lot and looking up toward the ornate faces that grew out of the revolving door's lintel. The middle one mocked him with its aggressive glare. As if it was daring Stew to try something. Stew stepped backward, shrinking beneath the face's glower.

He felt weaker and smaller than he had ever felt in his entire life.

What you've seen will drive you mad.

Unless you do something about it...

Stew inched away from the revolving door. He ducked his head down and placed his hands in his pockets.

But what could possibly be done?

He didn't even rightfully know what he had experienced.

Was the door a hungry mouth, or was it a portal leading to a fiendish lair?

Had the woman been eaten, or was she simply being digested? And how could Stew possibly help her? What could he even do?

He knew one thing... the door could lure people, like the pheromones that compelled an ant.

He hadn't just happened to grow so fixated on it... it had called out to him. It had pulled him in, and he had almost become trapped in it.

He was lucky to be alive, he realized.

Lucky to have even gotten away.

Stew didn't think of himself as a good man, or even a noble one. He had hurt a lot of people in his life... and yet he was compelled to take action.

TOXIC

He couldn't let another poor soul wander toward the revolving door the way he had.

Stew walked down the street until he came to a hardware store.

Stew waited diligently for it to grow dark outside.

It wasn't any less crowded on the streets as it would have been during the day... but he hoped that the shadows of nightfall would better conceal his identity if anyone cared to report what he intended to do.

Stewart Ripley had purchased a crowbar at the hardware store. A firm piece of metal with a sharp end that looked as if it could puncture glass easily.

He walked up to the revolving door swiftly, holding the crowbar toward the front of the vacant building so that no one would see it.

He very quickly stepped up to the space beneath the lintel and swung the crowbar.

The sound of glass shattering was as loud as a gunshot.

Someone down the street shrieked with surprise. He heard another person cheer, as if they were proud of his destructive act.

Stew swung the crowbar again, pulling the door with his free hand so that he could break all four of the revolving door's glass panels. The glass spider-webbed before giving in and crumbling.

He fit the crowbar through the opening of one panel and jerked it backward, hitting the doors frame until it was bent outward.

TOXIC

He pushed the door and the bent end caught against the wall. It refused to turn now.

Stew stepped back and smacked the metal faces with the toothy end of the crowbar until they were disfigured and clownish.

Then... Stew dropped the crowbar and ran.

A week after Stewart Ripley had destroyed the revolving door, he had kept his date with Felicia... and found it rather pleasant.

Felicia was not exciting or dangerous, but she was kind. And he also realized that he enjoyed the way she laughed. It was like the snuffling of a happy dog. So, he began to try and find new ways to crack her up, just to listen to the curious little noises she made.

They went out for dinner, and then a few days later they met up for brunch, and then a week went by, and they were making plans to spend a few nights together. He couldn't believe it, but Stew was actually taking the idea of dating Felicia seriously.

And he was thinking of Felicia was he rode the elevator up to his apartment on the last night of February. He was thinking of her smile and of her gentle voice, and he was becoming lost in a fantasy about their next date...

When the doors to the elevator opened.

Stewart wasn't at all surprised to see that the hallway leading to his room was occupied. There was usually someone milling about on their own way home. What surprised him was that they were standing by his door, as if they had come by for a surprise visit and were disappointed to find he wasn't home.

He squinted, worked up a smile, and stepped out of the elevator.

It was probably Layton and some friends...

But then, he noticed something was off about them.

For one, they were dressed in immaculate outfits. Victorian dresses for the ladies and a bright suit for the gentlemen.

Layton owned plenty of suits, but nothing this spectacular. It actually seemed to glitter, not unlike a disco ball.

"Who is that?" Stew asked as the elevator closed behind him.

The three visitors turned toward him and displayed wide smiles.

"You don't recognize us?" One of the women said.

"Who are you?" Stew asked and began to rifle through his pockets for his keys. "I'm sorry if I should know but—"

"You *should* know." The second woman said. Her voice was aggressive.

Stew felt his heartbeat quicken.

"You're the reason we couldn't finish our last meal." The man said.

He suddenly and horrifically recognized the three of them.

Two identical women with long hair... and a man with a gnarled beard and a row of almond shaped teeth. Each tooth ended in a sharpened point.

Oh, God. Stew thought.

The three spirits began to glide down the hallway. Their feet barely touched the ground. They glided like ghosts in Stew's direction.

He quickly slapped the button on the wall behind him and prayed that the elevator doors would open.

But even if they did, he knew that there was no escaping *them*.

They knew where he lived. They had found him. And he knew that they would never let him go.

"Please," Stew said aloud, "I could..."

"You closed our door on us." The man growled, baring his teeth. Stew noted that he had two fangs hidden just behind his canines, like the retractable teeth of a cobra. His purple tongue rolled along the curves of his fangs.

The women hissed in unison, brandishing their clawed hands. Each digit ended in a scarlet talon, about the length of a soda can.

Stew heard the elevator doors open... but the monsters were already upon him.

Stew screamed out as their claws ripped into his belly, and as their teeth sunk into different parts of his throat.

He expected them to drain him... but instead they pulled their mouths back and ripped his throat open. Ribbons of tattered tissue scurried down his chest. Blood jetted out, spraying the owlish faces of his assailants.

They pushed him back... into the elevator...

Only it was no longer an elevator...

...it was a long tunnel...

"We've opened a new portal, Stewart Ripley. Just for you..." The male said. "...just for you, and all your friends. We're going to drink deeply, Stewart. We're going to drink... *deeply*."

Stewart tried to scream one last time.

The sound bounced off the wet walls of the tunnel.

INNARDS-FUCK

"What is it?"

"It's a video."

"Is it real?"

"Nah. Maybe. I don't know." Dylan shrugged and looked back at his phone. "Yeah. It looks real."

On the screen, a man was holding his asshole wide open. Another man was impaling him with his amputated leg-stump. The sound of their friction was like two bullfrogs competing in a fart contest.

Dylan smiled and released a small giggle. "Ya never see a stump-fuck before?"

"No. Man. No." Fred shivered and looked back at his own phone. "That's crazy. Wouldn't that—like—destroy your guts?"

"Nah. The dude's an amputee. It's not like he's shoved his whole foot up that far." Dylan took a screenshot and then exited the site. He opened his messaging app and began to scroll idly through.

Dylan would have been handsome if he had ever actually given a shit. He had a sharp jawline, curly black hair, and a narrow nose. His eyes were small and beady, but they were magnified behind a pair of black rimmed glasses. He wore a hoodie with an anime-girl on its front, and he smelled like sweat and spices. His cheeks were acne scarred. A white pus-barrel was blooming between his left nostril and his lip.

Dylan Ashford was sixteen. A whole two years older than Fred Matheson. Fred didn't know why they were even friends. They were in different grades, watched different shows, and didn't even like the same music. Fred was into hip hop and Dylan's tastes were more experimental. Dylan listened to music that reminded Fred of white static and sandpaper massages.

They were sitting in the lunchroom at the end of the furthest table from the hallways. There were a few scattered loners sitting near them, but no one dared sit *by* them.

Fred and Dylan had convinced themselves that it didn't matter.

They didn't care about being popular—or likable.

Fred was a freshman. His face was round, and his blonde hair was overgrown. It fell down his shoulders in greasy strands.

He was wearing scuffed jeans and a black vest. He had been wearing the same outfit for four days straight now. He wanted to see how long he could go before people's eyes started to water around him.

"You wanna shoot up the school?" Dylan asked.

"Hey. Isn't that—uhm—illegal to say?" Fred retorted.

Dylan scratched his scalp and grinned. "I'm just kidding, buckaroo. Jeez."

"What if someone heard you?"

"I'll take you down with me. You're my co-conspirator."

Fred laughed and looked back toward his lunch tray. It was Pizza-Friday, and he was halfway through the cold slice. Back in elementary school pizza-day was an exciting event. Now it was just a chore to get through. He had enjoyed yesterday's greasy hamburgers more.

"We'll make a suicide pack." Dylan said through a mouthful of mushy carrots.

"We already have a suicide pact. And it's 'pact'. Not 'pack'." Fred stared Dylan down. "Don't you remember? Last week? You said we were gonna bomb the post office—"

"Oh yeah! And shoot each other afterwards." Dylan laughed and held his phone out. On it was a video from inside a toilet. "Watch this one."

"No. I'm eating." Fred insisted and looked down the table. There was a cluster of goths within earshot and a few computer nerds adjacent to them. Fred wondered if he and Dylan scared them. He hoped so. He liked being near Dylan, because it made him look intimidating—by proxy. Maybe that was why they had remained friends.

Fred didn't think anyone else would hang out with Dylan except for him. The kid was always getting in trouble and hadn't made much of an impression on his own class. He had been held back a year and was only a sophomore, despite being old enough to drive. Not that Dylan would even dream of getting behind the wheel of a car. He claimed he didn't want to drive because it would be all too easy for him to get the urge to squash a pedestrian. Fred knew that Dylan didn't drive because he was terrified, but he wasn't going to call his pal out on it.

"Hey, after school... I got something to show you." Dylan smirked.

"What?" Fred asked, turning his head back to his buddy.

"It's a movie." Dylan said. "You know how... you know how old man Schofield died last week?"

Everyone knew about it. The seventy-year-old geezer had been found in his bathroom with a knife in his throat. The murder of the geriatric was the talk of the town.

Dylan lived on the same block as the old codger. And—just as with his parents and schoolmates—the murder was all Dylan had been able to truly focus on. Their neighborhood was almost idyllic, and a murder had shocked that placidity.

"Man. If only I was paying attention that night! I could have watched it happen. You think he was... ya know... on the john? Like, *using* it? When it happened?" Dylan had mused a few days ago. He loaded up his slingshot and prepared to shoot a rock into the pond behind his house.

"I dunno. If you saw it happen, you'd tell the police, right?" Fred asked, watching the rock as it plinked through the pond's scummy surface.

"No. Who's to say old man Schofield didn't have it coming?" Dylan smiled with sick glee. "Maybe he was a freak or something. Maybe this was a 'revenge killing'."

Fred's theory was that some crazy had wandered in from the city and had decided to rob the geezer's house. Schofield wasn't exactly great at locking his doors. Fred's older brother—Rodney—had broken in once and lifted an antique watch just for a laugh. Of course, that was before Rodney had found Jesus and turned lame.

Fred then began to wonder whether or not his older brother had ever given the watch back.

Probably not.

That would have meant talking to Schofield... and no one liked doing that.

Schofield was a creepy dude.

He was like a living skeleton, and his eyes were so brown they looked black. His scalp was bald and scabby, and his nose was ruptured with sunburn scars. He spoke in a whisper too, which was extra creepy.

Fred had only met Schofield once.

It had been at a church barbeque, and it was a haunting experience.

Schofield had snuck up on Fred unannounced and laid a gnarled hand on his shoulder. His grip was tight, and he smelled like aftershave. Schofield leaned in close and said, "I saw you out by my woodshed last night. Best you keep away. Could get hurt."

"It wasn't me!" Fred stated defensively.

"I saw you." The old man sneered, released him, and slithered away. "I saw you."

Fred shook his head and drew himself back to the present. He looked at Dylan and cranked up a brow. "Yeah. I know about the murder. Everyone fuckin' does. What of it?"

Dylan mashed a fleshy piece of pizza-cheese into his mouth and smacked his lips. "I found something. You'll like it."

"Did you..." Fred started, shocked by the question on his mind. "Did you go into his house?"

"No. The police still have ticker-tape up. I don't want them dusting for prints and finding mine in there."

"Did you go in his woodshed?" Fred asked hesitantly. Recalling the grave warning Schofield had given him, Fred wondered whether or not he should have investigated the derelict shed after all.

Maybe there was treasure in there. Or money.

"No." Dylan shook his head and grinned. "But you'll see." He suddenly grew very serious. "I haven't shown this video to anyone yet. You'll be the first."

How ominous. Fred thought; reusing a word he had just learned in English.

The bell rang and the students began to filter out of the lunchroom and into the halls. As usual, Dylan and Fred waited until the lunchroom was empty before they left. They made it to their classes just before the tardy bell rang.

Fred tried not to think about Dylan's surprise, but it snuck into his brain at the most awkward of moments. He was thankful when their hours were up, and the students were headed toward their buses.

Dylan was waiting for Fred by the parking lot.

"C'mon, kid. We're skipping the bus and walking today. You ready?"

"Sure." Fred shrugged and wished he had left his schoolbag in his locker. He didn't feel like lugging it over his shoulder for the entire duration of their long walk home.

They made their way across the road and toward the apartment complex adjacent to the school. The road was paved but there were no sidewalks and barely a shoulder worth putting one's feet on. Fred stumbled behind Dylan.

"Do you know who Budd Dwyer was?" Dylan asked.

"No."

"He was a politician. I don't know much about him but, there's a video online of his death." Dylan spoke serenely, as if he was recounting the plot of his favorite television show. "I saw it awhile back. He's speaking at a press conference, and he pulls a gun out and shoots himself."

Dylan spoke with reverence, as if he was talking about an action movie hero.

Not a dead politician.

Fred realized that he understood Dylan about as well as most adults did.

Dylan's weird. He thought.

Then, he felt guilty. Everyone called Dylan weird, and Fred didn't want to be lumped in with everyone else.

TOXIC

"Huh." Fred stepped over a rock.

"It's crazy. The blood just, like, *poured* out of him. Like a waterfall out of his mouth and his nose. It's not like in the movies at all. It was like someone was squeezing a dishrag inside his head."

"Gross."

"Not gross." Dylan insisted, stooping over and picking up a stray stick. "Cool."

"Right." Fred pretended to agree. "Cool." Fred looked toward the apartments as they walked by them. An old lady sat on a lawn chair and watched them as they passed. She looked ill, with sallow skin and a snotty nose. Fred looked away from her and toward the sky, where blackbirds circled.

"Where are we going? Your place?" Fred asked.

"You'll see." Dylan laughed mischievously.

They passed the apartments, passed a few streets, and went the opposite way from both of their homes. It wasn't until they were approaching the gate that Fred realized they were coming up to the local cemetery.

"Wait." Fred froze and crossed his arms. "I thought you said we'd be watching a movie?"

"C'mon." Dylan dragged Fred toward the wrought iron gates. "It just feels better to watch it here."

"What are we watching it on? Your phone? I don't wanna watch a whole-ass movie on your phone in a graveyard, dude. And what if it starts raining? Seriously, man this sounds like—"

"It's only a couple of minutes. C'mon."

Dylan led Fred through the tombstones. They walked up a steep hill and stopped by an elm tree.

With the nonchalant briskness that was usually reserved for his house, Dylan tossed his school bag to the ground and plopped down onto his butt. He crossed his legs and pulled his phone out from his hoodie and began to scroll through his gallery.

"I went into my dad's computer last night." Dylan let the words sink in.

His dad was a cop, and sometimes Dylan liked to go onto his computer and look up crazy stuff.

He had figured out who the nearest pedophiles were and had made a sport out of egging their houses.

He had also brought crime scene photos to school to show to Fred and his pals—who tended to stop being his pals after seeing one crushed melon too many from the plethora of fatal car accident photos he kept in his backpack.

Whatever Dylan had found on his dad's computer, it was extra special.

It was something so disgusting and foul, he didn't want to advertise it.

He had chosen to show it to Fred in confidence.

Fred couldn't help but feel about as honored as he was sickened.

"What is it?"

"They already buried Schofield; ya know?" Dylan pointed ahead. Fred followed his finger and his eyes landed on a modest headstone. Franklin Sven Schofield had indeed been put into the earth. "I thought it was only fitting we watch this close by him."

Dylan patted the ground next to him.

TOXIC

Slowly, Fred took a seat by his friend and looked at the screen. Dylan had obviously recorded the video with his phone held up by his dad's computer screen. Dylan's toothy reflection was apparent in the corner. He looked absolutely gleeful.

Muffled by the tinny speaker on his phone, Dylan's voice chirped:

"I don't believe it. I don't believe it. Watch *this*."

The mouse appeared. A small, white speck that reminded Fred of spermatozoa. It clicked the black screen. The monitor was suddenly alight with shaky imagery.

"You never see his face." Dylan said in a hushed tone. "But he filmed it. Schofield did. Watch."

"I'm watching." Fred sneered and squinted. It was still bright outside and the image was hard to see.

The camera seemed to waver in the old man's hands. It struggled to frame a singular shot. Instead, it concentrated on random tidbits of imagery. A flattened beer-can, the dusty floor, the wooden walls. It was obvious to Fred that Schofield was recording this video from within his woodshed.

The large one behind his house. The one he warned me against entering.

Its interior was dark, musty, and barren. Except—

—except for the person suspended in its center.

Their arms were shackled together by a pair of fuzzy, pink handcuffs. The type of cuffs that Fred had found beneath his parent's bed—one afternoon after curiosity got the better of him—alongside a pile of dirty magazines and a dildo that looked too massive for use.

Fred shuddered and tried to take in more of the image.

The person was naked. Her breasts were saggy, and her stomach was round. She looked only slightly younger than the old man. Her face was obscured by a burlap sack, which had an oversized smiley-face sticker stamped directly on it.

The woman wavered from her handcuffs, which were secured above her with a leather strap. The strap was bound tightly around a wooden beam.

Schofield and the woman weren't alone. There was a man in there with them. Standing in the corner and massaging his cumbersome prick with a white hand.

The man was muscular and tall, and his face was hidden beneath a leather mask with a zipper-mouth.

"Do it." Schofield's familiar, soft voice rose up from behind the camera.

The masked man stepped up beside the elderly woman. He began to sensitively trace her stomach with his fingers. Fred could now tell that the man was young. Maybe in his twenties.

Fred's heart began to quake.

"Do it." Schofield wheezed.

The man reached out, and Schofield handed him something. Fred could see it for only a second. It was a hunting knife. A huge blade that was so shiny it looked as if the two men had passed a crescent moon from one hand to another.

"Watch this." Dylan said.

Fred had no choice. He couldn't look away, even though he wanted to.

The naked old woman was pissing herself. It came out in a hissing stream, which Schofield was quick to capture with his camera. He seemed more interested in her urine than he did the cavity the young man was carving into her side.

The knife slid in easily, tearing a simple hole into her belly. Blood poured out in a deluge, just as Dylan had described. Fred had expected a slow leakage, but the blood was watery and thin. It was like a red curtain being shaken loose. It streamed out of her and roared down her hip and onto the ground.

Schofield turned his camera up and zoomed in on the smiley-face bag. Fred was thankful they hadn't exposed her face. Instead, they just watched as the bag jerked itself back and forth.

The woman wasn't screaming.

Maybe she was incapable of it.

"Watch this."

At first, Fred thought it was Dylan, but he realized it was the masked man. Schofield turned the camera back toward the wound and brought it into focus. The man was fisting the hole. He had plunged his whole hand inside, and the fleshy lips of her wound were suckling his wrist. He drew his hand out, and a pulpy stew of feces and acrid fluids came out with it. Fred saw chunks of organ matter too.

The hand plunged back in and rootled around before returning with a stream of innards. *Long purple hoses which seemed to squirm as they were unearthed.*

"What is this?" Fred asked, nervously. "Is this... is this real?"

"Shhh." Dylan said.

The masked man took a wriggling tube and sliced it open with the knife. Gaseous air, blood, and intestinal droppings poured out of the hose. He dropped the knife. It landed on the dirt with a dull *thwack*.

Then, he positioned himself so that he could force his cock into the innards. He took the sliced hose and opened one of it into a dismal slit. With his hand gripping his shaft, he forced his cock into the organic cavity. He began to grind the tissues back and forth over the length of his glistening, purple-headed joint.

"Oh, God!" Fred stood up and backed into the tree. "Oh, God! Is he... is he...?"

Dylan began to laugh. "He's literally *fucking* her guts, dude!"

Fred covered his mouth with his hands. His face had gone red, and his stomach began to do cartwheels.

He wished he had never seen that video.

He wished Dylan hadn't led him into the graveyard.

He looked about in a state of panic. He wanted to be somewhere—anywhere—else. As far away from this creep and his demented video as humanly possible.

"No, but, dude, it isn't over yet... look!" Dylan shoved the cellphone into Fred's face.

Before Fred could beat the device away, he got a look at the frenzied freak fucking that poor woman's organs. His back was to the camera, and he had a detailed crucifix tattooed over his left hip. The irony was as stunning as the visual was disturbing.

Fred stamped away, leaving his book bag.

Dylan stayed beneath the elm, laughing maniacally.

"Fucking pussy! I thought you were cool, man!"

Fred didn't care. He didn't care what Dylan thought or said. He just wanted to go home.

Maybe I should tell.

Dylan's dad would definitely be pissed that he has that video. That's evidence, isn't it?

Fred shook his head. He didn't feel like telling.

He just wanted to forget about it.

Which, he worried, would be an impossible feat.

The walk home was long.

When he arrived, he sat in his bedroom and cried.

Afterwards, he went into the hall bathroom and forced his fingers down his throat.

Vomiting seemed to reduce his anxiety, but it did nothing for the guilt. Having watched that video made him feel as if he had taken part in Schofield's heinous activities.

After brushing his teeth and going to bed, he was surprised to hear a knock on the door. It creeped open before he could respond. Fred peered up and saw the silhouette of his older brother standing at the doorway.

"Hey, buddy. Are you feeling okay?" Rodney asked.

"Yeah." Fred turned over to hide his beet red eyes. "I'm fine."

Rodney walked in and sat down by him. He touched Fred's head. "You don't have a fever. I heard you yucking up and..."

"I'm fine." Fred insisted. "Just... Dylan and I had a fight."

"Oh." Rodney paused. "Well, I hate to say it but that might be for the best. I don't know about that kid."

Fred should have been defensive. But he didn't know how to be. So, he just shivered and curled his knees up to his chest.

"Wanna tell me about it?"

"No." Fred snapped. "Sorry. No. I just want to sleep."

"Okay. Well, if you need me, day or night, I'm there. I'm your big brother, and I love you. You know that, right?" Rodney stood and stretched. "And I'm praying for you. Things will turn out okay. Freshman year... I didn't know whether up was down. It took me a *long* time to figure life out."

"Thanks, Rodney." Fred turned over and smiled. "Thanks."

TOXIC

"Anytime."

Rodney rotated and walked toward the door.

He was shirtless.

Fred saw the tattoo of a crucifix on his back.

Rodney turned back toward Fred. The older brother smiled.

It was like looking into a shark's mouth. Fred felt his heart freeze in his throat.

"Pleasant dreams." Rodney slowly shut the door.

What Are You Going to Do with Me?

Sneaking around with his hoodie pulled over his head, Jack wondered if he looked like a creep.

Definitely. You totally do. And you are one. Stop pretending you aren't. Jack shuddered. He hated thinking so negatively about himself. But it was hard to deny the truth, no matter how unsavory.

He was a creep.

A pervert.

A total loser.

But... at least he was going to see some tits.

He hoped.

Jack looked over his shoulder and back through the woods. The van had been pulled over by the roadside. Standing on the edge of the forest, Linus had patted Jack on the back before saying:

"Sneak through the woods, climb the latticework on the side of the house... and I guarantee you'll spot some skin!"

Jack had swallowed a thick wad of saliva. "R-really?"

TOXIC

"Sure thing, bud!" Linus sniffled. It was October and he was just crawling over the hump of a massive head cold. The frat-house had been unnaturally quiet and still this last week, as everyone was doing their part to keep Linus unagitated and comfy. He was their king, and he was the most popular boy at Dearden... so when he was sick, it was as if the whole frat had fallen ill.

After getting better, Linus had decided it was about time Jack saw himself an honest-to-god rack of titty-meat. It had been a frequent point of conversation for the last few days.

It started with some light ribbing. Everyone knew that Jack was the only virgin left in Sigma Alpha Upsilon. He was the last of the recent crop of newbies to still have a beanie, which he was required to wear at all times in the house... and at parties. His pals and peers had all gotten laid, but girls were deterred by Jack.

In fact, if it wasn't for his dad's contribution to Dearden and his status as an SAU legacy, then Jack was sure he would've been kicked out with the rest of the losers that tried to crawl into the house during Rush Week.

In a moment of genuine concern, Linus cornered Jack in the communal bathroom and asked: "Why haven't you gotten laid? You a homo? It's okay if you are, bro. I mean, as long as you don't fag up the place. But, for real, are you?"

Jack went red. "No. No!"

"Thank Christ." Linus sneered.

TOXIC

Jack could tell he would've been ousted from SAU House is he *had* been gay. Legacy be damned. Politics be damned too. Linus and the rest of the frat brothers held several archaic prejudices. There was a reason why the skin surrounding Jack was milk-white...

"So, what's your deal, huh? You just don't like pussy or what?"

Jack shrugged. "I dunno. I've been... trying."

He had been trying hard. Jack went to every party and sniffed around every half-drunk or toasted girl he could find. Even in states of total inebriation, they rejected him.

At the last Sorority party, he had wandered into a room and found a girl collapsed on her bed. He could have had her—she was too drunk to complain—but she had vomited down her own chest. The slurry of bile and food chunks made Jack gag before leaving the room. Its acrid stink clung to his nose, reminding him of what could have been if he had simply pinched his nostrils shut...

But that would've been... assault.

He couldn't think the "R" word without his stomach curdling.

So? She wouldn't have known. No harm, no foul.
Unless it got out after I told my brothers.
Unless she woke up pregnant.
Unless... she somehow remembered it.

"I've been trying." Jack insisted, skirting around the dark thoughts in his cranium.

TOXIC

"Yeah, well... not hard enough. Look at ya!" Linus grabbed Jack by the shoulder and turned him toward the mirror.

Jack flinched.

His face was quilted in angry, white pimples. His beard was patchy. His upper lip was crusted with wiry hairs, some of which were ingrown. He was boney, his skin was greasy, and his knotty hair was cut short.

He could have cried.

When Jack was a child, he had imagined he'd be at peak performance in college. He had imagined himself a tall, handsome, and strong man. Instead, he was a five-foot tall loser, hanging out with superior men simply because his dad had jerked off in the same shower stall they washed their balls in when he'd been a younger man.

That's all I'll ever be. A footnote in my dad's life.

"You know, you remind me of myself." Linus huffed.

Jack raised a brow. "What do you mean?"

"I mean, I used to be an *uggo* back in high-school." Linus shrugged.

That just couldn't be true. Linus was muscled, smooth, and had the looks of a movie star. He was studying law, and from what Jack heard... he was good at it too. Linus had a bright future ahead of him, and an impressive body-count behind him too.

Linus had made it with every ten-point chick in every sorority circling their frat. He claimed that he'd stuck his dick so far down Monica

Guttenberg's throat, she'd thrown up into his urethra, blowing it up like a balloon!

Jack didn't know if he believed that aspect of the story, but he definitely believed that Linus had laid pipe with Guttenberg. She practically floated when he was around, like an angel in a cartoon.

There's no way he was ugly. Maybe he had a tricky pimple once or twice, sure... but there's no way he looked like me.

"Listen, weenie." Linus said, not unkindly. "I'm gonna crack ya a deal, yeah?"

"O-okay."

"You can keep the beanie off at the next frat party... if you sneak a peek at some tits. But you gotta promise me, you'll start hitting the gym and get into a good skincare routine. Because next year, you've gotta actually land some tail or I'll make sure *everyone* thinks yer a homo. Yeah?"

Nervously, Jack nodded. Then, he frowned. "Wait, what?"

"I'll let you off the hook as long as you see an honest-to-God boobie. And not on the computer. Or a strip club. And it can't be no prostitute either, cuz those skanks don't count. It's gotta be in the *flesh*." He drew the final word into an elaborate hiss.

Jack gulped. "How am I supposed to—I mean, I can't just *ask* a girl to show me her..."

"Why not?"

Jack flushed red. "They'll call me a creep."

"That's cuz ya are." Linus chuffed. "C'mon. I got an idea..."

TOXIC

Linus had kept his idea secret from Jack for the next few days. Eventually, Jack thought that Linus had forgotten all about their conversation. Then, Jack was jostled awake in his bunkbed.

He blinked and rubbed his eyes, taking in his surroundings. He thought that maybe he'd overslept and that one of his brothers was doing him a favor by rousing him. Then, Jack glanced toward the window and saw pitch darkness, pockmarked by stars.

"Huh?" Jack asked.

"C'mon, squirt." Linus said. He was dressed in black and wore a scuffed ski-mask. He looked like a robber.

Jack crawled off his bunk, being careful not to wake the boy beneath him.

"Get dressed." Linus tossed a bundle into Jack's arms. It was a black hoodie and a pair of black sweats. Jack slipped the clothing over his jammies. After dressing, he looked around the room. Part of him expected a herd of frat-bros, but it looked like whatever this was... it was between Linus and Jack.

"Follow me." Linus crept away and toward the door. He squeezed through the crack.

Jack came up behind him.

They inched down the stairs and out the back door. It was cold, and Jack was thankful that his pajamas kept him insulated underneath his hoodie.

They were a week away from Halloween, and this October had been cooler than most. The air felt soggy and frigid all at once. Jack wouldn't have been surprised to see snow and ice on the lawn.

He breathed through his teeth and followed close by Linus. He led Jack to his van and slid the door open.

Jack had never been allowed in Linus's van before. The vehicle was designated for beer runs, which Jack could never go on since he was only nineteen—the youngest boy in SAU—and didn't even know who to approach to get a fake ID.

Maybe Linus could help me out in that department.

Is he even helping you in the "titty department", or is this a ruse?

It struck Jack that this could be a trap. Maybe they were going to prank the last virgin standing from the new crop. An unspoken punishment for losing a game he didn't even know he was playing.

Jack crawled into the van, despite his worries.

"This the frosh, bro?" A voice piped up from the passenger-seat from the van's front.

Jack recognized Babe instantly.

Babe wasn't a member of their frat, didn't attend any of their classes, and he was in his mid-forties.

Yet, he was always around.

Especially at parties.

Tennessee "Babe" Olinger was a burned-out, bummed-out, whacked-out dude. His eyes were always red and hazy, and his belly was round from years of chugging. Jack figured that Babe drank more beer than water. The older man also had a nasty cough from the cigarettes and weed he continuously toked. Whenever he spoke, Jack imagined that Babe's throat was scabbed with rusty spikes.

How long as he been out here? Jack wondered, feeling uncomfortable. He'd never once been alone with Babe. The man was like a piece of furniture in the frat, but Jack had never spoken to him before, beyond a curt "hello".

"Yeah." Linus hopped into the driver's seat. "God! It's cold!" He pulled his ski-mask up, so it sat like a skull-cap above his brow. Linus's face was sheened with sweat and his eyes were teary. He rubbed his face with his hands and breathed harshly into his palms.

"Hey, you lookin' fer some titties tonight, huh?" Babe leaned back in his seat and spoke toward the rearview mirror.

Linus started the car and pulled away from the side-lot next to the frat house.

"Hey, kid. I asked ya a question. You wanna see some titties tonight or what?" Babe turned around and glowered at Jack. His face was scarred with acne and his beard was knotted. Babe made Jack feel like a million bucks when it came to looks.

And yet... Babe's pulling tail all the time. I've seen him walk out with drunk freshman at every party. How does he do it?

It's only cuz he buys 'em drinks. Bet all they ever do is jerk him off. He never sticks it in 'em.

Not like Linus.

The image of Monica Guttenberg vomiting on Linus's dick replayed in Jack's head.

"Y-yes." Jack said, finally answering Babe's vulgar question.

Babe grinned, like a fucked-up cherub. "Well, yer shit outta luck. You know this is a trap, right?"

Jack blanched. He felt needles crawl over his palms.

I knew it. But I got in the van anyways. Stupid. Stupid. Stupid.

Babe's smile expanded. It looked as if his head was about to break in half. "Linus lured you out here, so I could *rape ya!*"

Babe lurched forward, lunging toward Jack.

Jack was about to scream when Linus reached out and smacked Babe on the brow.

"Ow! Shit, dude!" Babe fell back into his seat. "I was jus' playin'."

"You're gonna make him shit himself."

"You knew I was jus' playin'. Shit. Coulda knocked my eye out."

Linus looked away from the road and into the back of the van. "You'll have to forgive Babe. He's an asshole."

"Yeah. Sure." Jack ground his teeth together. "I knew it was a joke." He didn't sound very convinced. "Just startled me, is all."

"Well, Babe ain't gonna rape you."

"Nah. I only rape chicks." Babe snorted.

Jack was certain that the old party-boy wasn't joking.

He might act like a goofball, but what would he have done if he found a passed-out girl all alone in a room?

TOXIC

Probably the exact thing I'd've done... only he wouldn't have been so finnicky about the puke.

Maybe that would've turned him one—

Oh, God! Don't think that!

Jack awkwardly coughed. He waddled up to the front seats and leaned in between Linus and Babe.

"So, where are we goin'?"

"A place that's guaranteed to get you exactly what you need." Babe said, cryptically.

"Where's that?" Jack asked.

"Jus' trust us." Babe insisted before fiddling with the radio. "Hey, Linus, you got this thing fixed?"

"Nah." Linus said. "You can plug your aux cord in though."

"The fuck's an aux cord?" Babe muttered. "You got any CD's."

"No one does." Linus chuckled. "Get with the times, old man."

"Hey! You respect yer elders. I can still drink yer white ass under the table."

"Your ass is whiter."

"Yeah? How'd you know?"

Jack settled back onto his rump, listening to the two guys argue and joke. The easy way they talked reminded Jack of his pals back home.

Real friends.

I don't have any real friends in SAU.

Not unless you count my right hand.

She's always been good to me.

Jack almost laughed aloud at his own joke. He stifled it and focused on his hands.

TOXIC

In no time at all, the van shuffled to the side of the road. Linus pulled the keys and flicked off the headlights. Babe lit another smoke and puffed angrily, as if he was trying to win an argument with his cigarette.

"We're here." Linus said, tugging his mask back over his head.

Babe popped the glove compartment open and rootled around in Linus's stash of roadmaps, papers, and bottles. He exhumed a ski-mask and slipped it over his own dome.

"Where are we?" Jack asked.

Neither of the men answered.

Instead, they opened their doors and stepped out of the van. Jack waited for the door to slide open. When it did, he marched out on rickety legs.

"Sneak through the woods, climb the latticework on the side of the house... and I guarantee you'll spot some skin!" Linus said, clapping Jack on the back. A little too hard. Jack wavered on his feet but suppressed a frightened yelp.

Jack swallowed a thick wad of saliva.

"R-really?"

"Sure thing, bud."

"Who's house is it?" Jack asked.

"Does it matter?" Babe snorted. "Tits 'r tits."

Jack shuddered. He hoped they weren't pranking him. What if he looked in the window and spotted an old lady, with breasts like pancakes on her chest?

Tits 'r tits. Yeah, right. Not all tits are created equal, dude.

TOXIC

Jack looked over his shoulder and back through the woods. He could see the hulking shadow of the van, but he had no idea what Linus and Babe were up to.

They're probably gonna sneak up behind me and scare me.

Just for fun.

Jack needed to get out of his own head.

He turned his tongue over between his teeth. Biting down on the muscle relieved him of his train of thought, if only for a moment.

Jack snuck through the woods. Fallen leaves crunched beneath his feet. A cold wind crept through the trees, rattling their dried branches. Knotty fingers poked through the shafts of moonlight that illuminated Jack's path.

He came to the edge of the forest and hunkered down behind a bush. Peering through the foliage, he saw the house. *It's pretty nice.* Jack thought. *But anything looks okay after you've spent a long enough time in a greasy frat.*

It was a two-story abode, equipped with ivy-coated latticework, and wide windows. The lights were on in the top story. Piss yellow and glowing.

Jack considered his options. He'd be trespassing, plus he'd be labeled a pervert if he was caught. Also, he had never climbed a lattice before. Would it hold?

Just do it. If you don't, Linus will be super disappointed. He'll make your life a living hell.

TOXIC

He'll probably keep his word and spread a rumor that you're a homo.

Jeez.

Feeling like a creep, Jack snuck out across the lawn. He worried that his presence would trigger an automatic set of lights, but he was safe in the dark. The wind kicked his hoodie back. He gnawed on his lower lip as he leapt across the lawn and crouched down by the air conditioning unit beside the lattice.

Whoa. You're just a couple steps away from becoming an official peeping tom! Congrats, loser.

Shut up.

Jack stood and hooked his fingers through the square nocks of the lattice. The wooden structure seemed to rustle, but one tug proved it to be firm.

Am I really about to do this? Jack wondered as he hefted his weight up. *I already am.*

He wheezed, grunted, and hissed as he went up the lattice. He tried to be quiet, but the climb was a struggle. In the movies, they always set a tree right beside the window, so the pervert didn't have to bother himself too much.

Jack remembered Jon Lovitz as the peeper in *Little Nicky*.

He had had a comfy, cozy spot on a tree, which provided him with a front row seat to the show—

But then he fell, died, and went to Hell.

Jack supposed he'd never laugh at that scene again.

TOXIC

I bet most creeps don't think about Adam fuckin' Sandler movies while they're perving on innocent women.

Jack wondered why he wasn't backtracking. He could just tell Linus he saw a boob and that would be that. It wasn't as if Linus was here with him, just to confirm that Jack wasn't fibbing.

You're stepping over a line here. Whoever this girl is, she didn't sign up to be ogled. Especially in her own home.

What are you, a feminist?

That's almost as bad as being gay.

Jack had once heard Linus talk about beating up on queer kids in high-school. At first, it had seemed funny. Jack's views aligned with his peers at the frat. People were too soft nowadays and needed a bit of bullying to "straighten" them out.

Of course, this was easier *thought* than *experienced*.

If Jack was being bullied, he doubted he'd like it very much.

He was up to the window now.

Jack sucked in a long breath.

The wind hit him, and his heart lurched in his chest as he swayed with the breeze. He imagined losing his footing and screaming all the way down.

It was a two-story drop. He wouldn't die... but he could break a leg. Then, he'd have to deal with the panicked homeowners, ushered out by his shouts.

He had to be careful.

He had to be cautious.

TOXIC

Biting into his lower lip, Jack leaned toward the window and peeked in.

He was surprised by the warmth of the room. The bedspread was pink, and the walls were decorated with movie posters. There was a burbling fish tank, and the creatures inside appeared tropical and expensive.

A house in the middle of the woods? Of course, it's owners are probably wealthy.

Another layer of discomfort swaddled Jack. He realized that this looked like the room of a teenager.

Sure, he was only nineteen... but how young was the girl that lived here? Was she in middle school?

Had Linus and Babe set Jack up to look like a pedophile?

He was relieved when the woman walked into the room. She was young, yes... but not *too* young. Probably around twenty or twenty-three.

She was tall and narrow. Her eyes were creased, and her skin was glazed with moisture.

She walked in with a robe on and a towel around her head.

Jack was confused by the serendipitous nature of what he was witnessing.

She probably has a nightly ritual. Linus and Babe know about it. He realized that he was breathing heavily, and that his erection was prodding the side of the house. He wiggled his hips and adjusted his grip on the lattice.

The woman pulled her towel away from her head, exposing a boyish flash of red hair. She ran her towel through her hair thoroughly before tossing it into the hamper, which squatted beside her closet doors.

All of Jack's doubts and worries slipped away from him. Entranced by what he was seeing, he forgot all about the morale quandary he had placed himself in. He forgot that what he was doing was wrong—a violation. All he could think was that *it* was finally happening.

He was about to see the real deal. And not secondhand through a computer screen. He was going to see a naked woman... in the flesh!

And as long as I don't fall, it'll be like I'm not even there. It'll be like... I'm just a ghost.

She'll never know that she shared her secrets with me.

She didn't take her robe off. Instead, she sat down on the edge of her bed, stretched like a cat, and flopped back. Her robe rode up her legs, exposing her slickened thighs. They seemed to sparkle.

She rolled over, facing away from the window. Her robe shuffled up, exposing the cleft of her rear.

Jack's jaw could've hit the ground.

His eyes grew huge in their sockets, as if they were being filled with a bicycle pump.

She rolled back, turning her head toward the ceiling.

That was when her door thumped open.

Jack was so shocked he almost let go of the lattice.

He watched as a handsome man strode into the room, holding a towel around his own hips.

They were showering... together!

"I love that look on you." The man's voice was muffled through the window.

"What? This look?" She spread her legs.

Jack couldn't see anything. The angle of her legs was all wrong. But the man's reaction was imprinted on the front of his towel.

"Jesus, Bonnie!" The man scratched the back of his head. "We just got cleaned up!"

"Well, I might wanna get dirty again." Bonnie laughed.

"That work on all the guys or just me?" The man rolled his eyes. Then, he dropped his towel.

Jack felt guilty looking at his penis, but it was too impressive to ignore. It looked like a swollen root lodged at the bottom of his sturdy pelvis.

"Everything works on you." Bonnie said.

The man shrugged before striding toward the bed. His cock led him.

Bonnie swallowed it greedily.

Holy fucking shit!

She languished on his rod, taking it into her throat and nuzzling his pubic mound with her nose.

The man closed his eyes and rolled his head back.

She spread the bottom of her robe open and... reached down. Down between her thighs, where her secret was kept.

Show it to me. Show it to me. Jack thought fervently.

He almost wished they would catch him.

He imagined a porno scenario, where the man dragged Jack into the room and said:

"You wanna know what it feels like, huh? Well, have at her!

That was stupid though. That only happened in make-believe.

If they saw him, this lunkhead would probably strangle him.

Her other hand cupped the man's scrotum. She seemed to roll his balls around in her hand like they were a set of marbles.

He pulled away. His cock was slickened with her saliva.

Jack wondered how her spit smelled.

"You really wanna fuck again, Bonnie?" The man asked.

"I do." She said, working her hand between her legs.

"Well, it'd be rude of me not to." He joked.

Quit talking and get it on!

Jack felt a line of drool fall out of his mouth. His grip on the lattice was white-knuckled.

The man stooped down, grabbed Bonnie by the hips, and pulled her toward the edge of the bed. He buried his face between her legs, lapping at her sex with an eager tongue.

Jack could almost taste her through the window. He wondered if she released the exact same musky stink that Linus had bragged about smelling from Monica Guttenberg's crotch. Jack wondered if all girls smelled the same when they got excited, or if each one had a unique flavor.

TOXIC

"Girls always leave a little stench on ya. It's like a stamp." Linus had once explained to Jack. "You know it's a good fuck if yer dick smells a bit like raw fish afterwards—"

Speaking of Linus, there he was.

Jack's mind was boggled by what he was seeing. He figured he was hallucinating.

There was no way Linus was striding into the room, holding a knife in both of his hands.

Bonnie's eyes were closed, and the man was busy working at her cunt with his mouth. They didn't notice anything was wrong until the blade *thunk*-ed into the man's skull.

Linus fell onto his victim, pressing the man's face into Bonnie's pelvis, trapping her against the bed. The man was sandwiched between the frat boy and his screaming girlfriend.

Bonnie's robe fell open as she fell against the bed, but Jack couldn't look at her. His eyes were affixed to the knife, which had punched through the back of the man's skull. Its shiny tip protruded just below the man's left eye. It left a zig-zag of bloody cuts down Bonnie's thigh as she dragged herself away from the pileup.

Linus stood, straddling the man and dragging him up to a sitting position by the foot of the bed. The man was dead. The weapon had scrambled his brains before poking through his.

Pulling on the handle like a lever, Linus made the man nod lazily. Blood gushed out of the man's mouth and spattered the bedspread, which was rumpled by Bonnie's movements.

Linus was grinning maniacally through his ski-mask. His teeth were white and sharp.

This can't actually be happening. Jack thought. *I must've fallen and hit my head. This is some hallucination, and I'm in a coma. I'll wake up in a hospital bed, surrounded by my frat brothers. Far away from this—*

Bonnie raced around the room, pumping her arms. She was covered in her boyfriend's blood. It stained her creamy flesh and darkened her red hair. Jack watched as she plowed through the door.

He heard her scream.

Babe dragged her back into the room, an arm looped around her throat and a hand gripping one of her joggling breasts.

Jack felt frozen. He wanted to knock on the window and demand that Babe let the woman go. He wanted to plead with Linus in the hopes that he could somehow revert the terrible violence he had just brought down onto this innocent man.

"Damn! You didn't have ta kill him so fast!" Babe barked as he wrestled Bonnie toward the bed. She gurgled against his arm and beat her hands beside him. Her attacks were weak. She was too stunned and terrified to defend herself.

Her eyes glanced from Linus to the arm lashed around her.

Babe continued to squeeze her breast.

His fingers left deep gouges and purple bruises on the surface of her flesh.

"You see this guy? Linus said. "He's huge." He yanked the knife out of the man's head. Without

Linus's support, the man careened to the ground. He was curled into a fetal ball at Linus's feet. Blood seeped out of where the knife had penetrated and exited his head.

"Yeah, but it woulda been fun to make him do stuff to her." Babe reasoned. His hand swept down and clutched the crying woman by her vagina. His fingers buried themselves into her slit.

Bonnie's sobs turned into high-pitched shrieks.

"We'll do enough to her. We don't need company." Linus said, striding toward Babe and Bonnie.

He wiped his knife clean on an unbloodied section of her robe.

"Hold her yapper open."

"No! No!" Bonnie roared.

Babe gripped her jaw and tugged.

"No!" Bonnie gurgled.

Linus worked his fingers into her mouth and grabbed her tongue. He yanked it—*hard*.

Bonnie's screams became higher pitched as he took the blade and laid its edge on her tongue. Slowly, Linus dragged the knife down the length of the muscle, slicing it right down the middle.

Jack felt his gorge rise as he watched the tongue split in two. Blood flew out of the wound as Bonnie thrashed and bucked against her captors.

"Fuckin' A, bro!" Babe hollered.

He tossed Bonnie onto the bed. She scrabbled around on its bloody surface, moaning and crying. One of her white hands held her mangled tongue, which flopped around between her pearly teeth.

The other hand grabbed up the blanket and pulled it closer to her chest.

This is evil.

Why are you watching this?

You could run.

Get the police.

Tell them... tell them it was Babe and Linus.

Then you'd have to admit you were peeping.

Fuck it!

Who cares?

What they are doing is way worse than voyeurism!

Babe grabbed the neck of Bonnie's robe and wrenched it back with an animalistic grunt. She was jerked upright, and her arms pedaled by her sides.

Linus held his knife in his mouth and helped his pal tear the robe away from Bonnie. Completely exposed, Bonnie shriveled into her bed. She held her arms over her breasts and pinched her legs shut.

"Please! Please, let me go! Y-you don't have to! *You don't have to!*" Bonnie shouted.

Linus was first. He raped her for what felt like an hour but was—in truth—only a few minutes.

Jack watched as Linus drove himself into her. He watched as the knife sawed at her neck-flesh, spreading the skin open but not digging in deep enough to nick an artery.

Bonnie screamed the whole time.

After Linus was done, Babe took his turn.

While Babe grunted between Bonnie's legs, Linus used the knife to cut her robe into strips, which he then applied to her arms and legs. Before long, Bonnie was tied down to the bedposts.

Linus did this, all while Babe thrust in and out of her.

When Babe was finished, he stood and admired his work.

Bonnie was slicked with crimson blood. Her thighs were scrabbled with knife-scratches. Her throat was cut. Her tongue was tattered, and her mouth was filling with blood from the wound. She tilted her head to the side and a red strand slipped out of her oral cavity and landed on the pillow beside her head. Linus and Babe's semen glimmered on her belly and oozed between the lips of her battered cunt.

"Punch her a couple times." Linus said.

"Okay, boss." Babe replied.

He turned her head upright, then pounded it with his fists. He beat her nose so hard it shattered like a broken vase. Blood spouted from the rumpled flesh and filled the air around her.

"That's enough." Linus said.

Babe stepped back, obedient to his master.

Bonnie's left eye was swollen.

Babe's punch had ruptured the right eyeball, and it was filling with red blood.

"How much of her boyfriend do you think she can eat?" Linus asked.

"I dunno." Babe said. "But I'd like to find out."

Linus knelt down and punched the knife into the dead man's tummy. He recoiled as a swampy burble escaped the wound.

"God, I always forget about how they stink." Linus muttered before returning to work.

He cut out a length of rubbery intestine. Leaving the knife embedded in the corpse, Linus walked over to the side of Bonnie's bed and grabbed her by the throat.

"Open." He commanded.

Bonnie wheezed and rasped, but her wounds were too egregious to allow her to properly communicate with her captors. Jack doubted she could think, much less comprehend what Linus was saying.

"I said... *OPEN*!" Linus began to shove the intestinal tissue against Bonnie's mouth.

The taste of the organ-matter seemed to rouse her. She opened her mouth to scream, and Linus pressed the dredged-up innards down her hatch.

She coughed, sputtered, bucked, and brayed, but Linus was determined to make her eat.

"Cut more off of him!" Linus shouted.

Babe went to work.

He returned with the man's severed penis.

"Think she can swallow it whole?" Babe asked.

"Nah. I got a better place fer that." Linus said and pointed between her legs.

They pushed the dismembered cock into her like a squishy dildo. All the while, Bonnie continued to weep, cough, and scream.

TOXIC

They fit as much of the man into her as they could. Babe removed his lungs, and they laid them atop her chest and told her to keep still. When she disobeyed and the lungs fell to her sides, Linus was quick to punish her.

He forced the swollen flesh around her good eye open and used the tip of the blade to pop her eyeball. Warm liquids gushed out of the purple crater that had once been her socket.

Then, he took the man's eyes and laid them over Bonnie's leaking sockets. It looked like her eyes were bugging out of her skull.

Jack watched this from outside the window. He had grown numb with shock and horror. He couldn't believe what he was watching, and yet he refused to look away.

It was disgusting... disturbing... and terrifying.

He knew he should be running, but he couldn't. His impulse was to stay and watch.

He watched... and watched...

When Babe and Linus were done, they met Jack at the bottom of the lattice. He climbed down cautiously, shivering in his shoes.

"You wanna go up and take a look at her?" Linus asked.

"Yeah. Seeing is one thing... but touching? Now, that's the real article!" Babe chuffed.

Jack's face must have looked gaunt, because Linus frowned and said: "Hey, sorry if this freaked you out, bud. We just wanted to give you a show, ya know?"

TOXIC

Jack found himself nodding. "I know. I know. I was just—"

What could he say? That he was appalled? That he couldn't believe that Linus would do something like that? That there must not be a God because what sort of sick fuck creates a universe were... *that*... was permitted?

Instead, Jack swallowed harshly and held his own chest.

"We won't peek in on you or nothing." Linus said. "You just go up and spend a little time with her, uh-huh?"

"O-okay." Jack said, unsure if he had any other choice in the matter.

Babe lit another cigarette and puffed deeply. He had stubbed out two lit smokes on Bonnie's belly after his third round between her legs was spent. Jack wondered how many cigarettes were left in his pack.

"Just go in, man. You'll understand it when you are alone with her." Linus insisted, holding the sliding glass backdoor open.

Jack trudged into the house on heavy feet.

He marched up the steps and walked down the hall leading to the bedroom.

It stank like a zoo.

Musky.

Bloody.

Shitty.

Jack pushed the door open with his shoulder and took in the sights.

From another angle, the room looked even worse than it had through the window.

The carpet was soggy with blood.

The boyfriend's head was floating in the fish tank. Bonnie's tropical pets nibbled at the ragged stump below his chin.

Tied to the bed, Bonnie was an atrocious sight.

Her vagina was curdled with sperm, blood, and strands of tissue from her boyfriend's torn penis.

Her belly was a network of scratches and slashes. Some of the gouges went deep. A thin membrane grew over these harder wounds.

Her left cheek had been seared away from her face, exposing the rear of her jaw.

Her front teeth had been knocked loose from her gums by Babe's punches.

Jack swallowed and looked toward her chest. Her breasts had been left uninjured—aside from the cuts and bruises caused by Babe's sloppy fingers. They were the only part of her that Linus's knife hadn't touched.

Bonnie wheezed sharply and wetly. It sounded like a hiss cockroach.

Jack's heart leapt into his throat, and he stepped back.

"Puh... puh-*leeeeze*... stop..." She shook her head, as if she was waking up from a nightmare.

"Hey, hey—it's okay. I'm not gonna hurt you."

She turned her head toward him. One of her boyfriend's eyes fell out of her socket and plopped against the bed. She breathed erratically.

Panicked. Hurt. Scared.

TOXIC

"I'm not... I'm not going to hurt you." Jack's eyes fell back onto her breasts.

In spite of the blood, the gore, the pain, and the trauma... his dick began to rise in his pants. It pressed against his thigh, swelling with excitement.

He remembered the drunk girl.

He had regretted not doing anything to her... even though he knew that doing stuff with her would've been wrong.

But he had never had a real opportunity to do anything with anyone...

Until now.

No! He couldn't even humor it.

And yet... he thought of what would happen after this.

Linus had told Jack to get in better shape, and that he'd need to figure out his sex life before he turned into an object of ridicule.

What if... Jack could skip the whole ordeal?

What if he dealt with the problem now?

Besides, what did Bonnie care?

Compared to his pals, Jack could be gentle with her.

Maybe she'd even like it.

One last, loving screw before her heart gave up and she drifted over the vale and into the hereafter...

She was going to fuck her boyfriend tonight anyways. So, what difference did it make?

Jack licked his lips.

"I'm... I'm not going to hurt you."

A beat of silence crossed between them.

TOXIC

Her voice tinged with fear, Bonnie asked: "W- what are you... going to do with me?"

Toxic

Polly knelt down by Tucker and took his face in her hands. She did this when she needed his full attention.

"What are we *not* going to do?" Polly asked our eight-year-old son.

"Swim too far."

"What are we *going* to do?"

"Stay where mama can see me." Tucker's cheeks went red.

I felt a bit bad for the tyke, but I was also aware that Polly's protectiveness was valuable. A boy needed a balance between a father's acceptance and a mother's care, and I think Tucker got an even measure of both.

We were in the hotel room, which had a sliding glass door that led right onto the sandy beach. The beachfront resort was gorgeous, ritzy, and well out of my budget. I was thankful that the company had paid for my stay. That meant that this wasn't an *actual* vacation, but I only had a few meetings to attend. That meant I'd be spending more time with my son and wife, with only a few hours of work-required distance. Besides, I'm sure they would appreciate the respite from my "dad jokes" whenever I went to my morning meetings.

I was just as excited to go to the beach as Tucker was. Although, being a grown-up, I was more interested in lounging on the sand and soaking up the sun. I worked in an office, so my skin was so white it blended in with the walls of my cubicle. I was hoping to return home with a tan.

I also had a paperback thriller stowed away in my wife's beach-bag. It was something I had picked up at the airport during our connected flight. I didn't really know what it was about, but it had a familiar name on the cover along with an image of a plane falling nose-first through the sky.

I hadn't read a book for fun in *years*. I hoped I could make some headway through it before we had to pack up, board our plane, and return to our home in Missouri.

I walked up to the glass door and slid it open. Instantly, the salty air from the sea seeped into our room. I took a deep breath, pulling in the ocean's spicy scent. I closed my eyes and listened. I could hear kids laughing, sand shuffling, and the gentle *rustle* of waves lapping at the shore.

I turned back to Tucker and Polly. She was helping our child put on his inflatable water wings. Tucker was a pretty good swimmer, but Polly didn't like to take chances.

"Hey, gang." I spoke.

Both my wife and my son looked toward me. I bet I was a sight to behold with my skinny, pale legs, my pot belly, and my tacky Hawaiian shirt. My hair didn't do me any favors either. It had grown stringy and gray lately.

"So, my meeting goes until eleven tomorrow... wanna go to Disney after I'm done?"

Polly smirked. We had already planned our trip to the theme park, but we'd kept it secret from Tucker. The little boy's face broke into the sort of glee children usually reserve for Christmas.

"Honest?" He asked, his eyes agleam.

"Scouts honor." I crossed my heart.

Tucker raised his arms above his head and whooped loudly. I could see that Polly had only managed to fit one floatie onto his left arm. His right was bare. She struggled to bring the limb back down and fit the inflatable onto it.

My fault, I'd gotten him riled up. I'd been working on Tucker ever since we told him we were going to Florida. I'm sure, to him, this place was a dream come true. I'd built it up to be heaven on earth, with my stories of crystal-clear water, crazy wildlife, and theme parks.

This vacation was a godsend.

I'd realized awhile back that I hadn't taken my family on trips the way my dad did when I was a kid. Back in the day, we had traveled nearly to every corner of the United States before I left for college. Those trips had been downright whimsical, and I still looked back on those memories with overwhelming fondness.

And yes, we went to Florida when I was a kid. I remember my dad renting us a yacht. We spent the night on the ocean, fighting sea sickness and

TOXIC

listening to his stories of underwater monsters. Even today, I get shivers when I hear the word "Kraken". I always imagine my dad's salty, raspy, smoky voice telling us all about the tentacled fiend, and how it was known to wrap itself around boats and pull them deep into the depths...

Funny how certain things from one's childhood can both traumatize you and fill you with nostalgia all at once.

I didn't think I'll be repeating my dad's scary sea stories to my son. Tucker's a fairly delicate kid, and if I told him about a tentacled beastie lurking under the water, then he'd probably spend the entire week locked in our room with the blinds blocking out the Floridian sun.

"Whats yer favorite ride at Disney, Dad?" Tucker asked while his mother lathered his face with a protective layer of sunscreen.

"Oh, I dunno, sport. It's been so long since I've been there. Heck, I was probably about your size when my Pa took me!" I reached over and ruffled his hair. "I bet it's all changed since then. That was about eight-hundred and eighty-eight years ago!"

Polly giggled a little louder than Tucker.

We were young parents. I was cresting the last months of twenty-nine, while Polly was barely over thirty. We had gotten committed early and had Tucker right off the bat. Most of my chums in high-school were still "trying to find themselves". I had it figured out. I'd work an office gig to support what really mattered, and that was my family.

Someone walked by our opened door. They were lugging an old fashioned boombox on their tattooed shoulder, and the radio was playing tinny surf music. You couldn't have asked for a better ambiance!

"Okay, kiddo. Let's hit the beach!" I declared, surprising Polly.

"He's not ready yet!" She started, but it was too late.

Tucker raced to my side and danced by the sliding door. I gathered Polly's beach bag and inspected its innards. Towels, sunblock, bagged snacks, extra sunglasses, my thriller paperback and her horror novel—I don't know how she read that stuff without getting nightmares. I looked back toward my wife and gave her a grin.

"We're ready! How about you, slow-poke?"

This earned a chuckle from Tucker and a sardonic glare from Polly. She stood, grabbed her sunhat, and walked over to meet me and our son by the door.

"I guess I'm ready if you are." She sighed.

I gave her a peck on the cheek. My wife was beautiful. Round faced, brown haired, and freckled like a sun-bleached pear. I suddenly wished that we had two rooms so we could catch some privacy. But our bed and Tucker's were side-by-side. Even with the company forking over the dough for our beachside lodging, this wasn't *exactly* a Hilton. Still, it was a step fancier than what I could have afforded on my own.

We'll get some alone time once we're back home. Maybe we'll make Tucker a little brother. I thought, and I hoped the mesh lining of my trunks was holding my sudden erection back. Last thing I wanted was for a surfer to point at me and shout "shark!" if I decided to jump in for a backstroke.

"Should we bring water bottles and—" Polly started.

"There's a hot dog stand over on the beach." I said. "I was gonna pick us up some dogs and sodas."

"Tucker shouldn't swim immediately after eating. He'll get a cramp an—"

"I'll get him a dog after he finishes swimming." I corrected myself, giving him a wink. "With extra relish!"

"Yuck." Tucker muttered.

"You'll like it when you're grown." I quipped.

"If being a grown-up means eating green slime... count me out!" Tucker brayed.

My wife and I both laughed.

The three of us stepped out onto the concrete porch beyond our room. I caught sight of a green lizard basking on the ground, unworried and slithery. I thought about making a joke about putting it on a hot dog for Tucker, but he could get a little sensitive about animals. Polly and I both theorized that he'd become a vegetarian if we told him what hamburgers and hotdogs were made from.

TOXIC

We strolled toward the beach. The rising dunes separating the resort from the water were as round as lumps of ice cream. And just as smooth.

I saw babes and hunks stretched out on blankets.

I could see a parasailer wafting over the water behind a speeding boat.

Steam was rising up like a beacon from the hot dog stand.

It was heavenly.

Being from Missouri, the beach held an otherworldly quality. It reminded me of those old sci-fi movies, when the cast took their first steps out of the spaceships and took in the unnatural yet beautiful sights around them.

"Ouch!" Tucker yipped.

I looked down and saw he had managed to get out of the room with bare feet. He danced on the hot sand. Swiftly—and before Polly could shout for me to act—I scooped Tucker up and maneuvered him onto my back. He wrapped his arms around my neck and breathed heavily into my ear. He wasn't rushed or panicked, but his breath was relieved.

"Sand's pretty hot!" He exclaimed.

"Yeah. You gotta watch out, or it'll sting ya!" I said, laughing.

Polly reached around me to pat our son on the back. "You okay, pudding? Want me to go grab your sandals?"

"Nah. I'm good." Tucker said. "'sides, I'll be in the water soon!"

"You never know." I joked. "The water could be boiling! You'll turn as red as a lobster after I dunk you in it!"

"Dad!" I could tell he was rolling his eyes.

I gave Polly a sly smile, and she returned it with a wink.

As a family, we walked toward the beach. We had to weave through crowds of lounging surfers, tourists, and sunbathers. Eventually, we found a spot to rest. Polly laid out a beach blanket, and I walked Tucker toward the water.

"Ya wants me ta launch ya?" I asked in a chipper tone.

"Yeah!" Tucker shouted.

"Now, you remember to pinch your nose and keep your mouth shut, yeah? The water is salty. It tastes like bad eggs."

"Yuck!" Tucker stuck his tongue out.

"Yuck, for sure." I said.

I waded in up to my waist. It was more water than I wanted, and the salty sea was cold around my pelvis. I helped Tucker around from my back to my front. He planted his sand caked feet in my palms, and I heaved him up into the air. He yelped as he flew through the air before crashing into the water. Spittle sprayed around his point of impact. I heard a woman hiss with revulsion before marching away.

If you didn't wanna get wet, ya shouldn't have gotten into the water! I thought, glancing toward the woman.

TOXIC

Tucker came up from the water with a cheer. "Again! Again!" He paddled toward me rapidly.

By the time I had convinced him I was too tired to play "launch pad" any longer, I had thrown Tucker into the water about fifteen times in a row.

I walked up on the beach, collecting sand on my wet feet as I went. Polly already had her horror novel open, but she set it down to hand me a towel, which I used to pad my sandy toes.

"You want a hot dog?" I asked.

"No. I'll wait." Polly responded, putting her eyes back on the pages.

I scoped out the cover with a shudder. The front of the book featured a teddy bear with a massive hook through it, set under a set of leering eyes. The title was *The Groomer*, and it was by some guy that called himself "Jon Athan". I smirked at the funny pseudonym. *At least the guy has a sense of humor. You'd have to have a couple jokes up your sleeves if you are going to write all that sick shit.* I couldn't help but judge my wife's taste in literature. She would read about children being abducted and murdered, and then she'd over-worry about our own son afterwards.

"That's why you're so nervous all the time." I said as I dug into her beach bag for my thriller.

"Hmm?" She looked over with raised brows.

"You read those books, and it makes you nervous." I said. "Maybe you should try something nicer. Hell, even Stephen King isn't as scary as the stuff you read."

Polly laughed. "I like King! He's plenty scary!"

TOXIC

"I like his normal stuff. Not the early ones. I like a good mystery... not rabid dogs and killer clowns." I acted like I was shivering.

"Your problem is... you're a pussy." Polly sniped.

Both of us laughed at the vulgarity. As much as we chided each other, it was always good natured. I could scoff at her choice of literature all I wanted, but there wasn't a single thing I'd have changed about my Polly.

I wriggled up beside her. Our hips touched, sending an electric thrill through me.

"You wanna take turns watching Tucker?" I offered.

"Yeah. Sure." Polly said.

"I'll go first. You read your gore-porn."

"Har-har." She chittered.

I watched my son play in the water. His energy was boundless. I was sure that Disney would only ratchet up the vigor. We'd have to run to keep up with him by the time we stepped through the gates of the Magic Kingdom.

I heard a scream.

Not an unusual sound at the beach, but the tone drew my eyes away from my kid and down the sandy landscape.

I couldn't see who had screamed, so I found my gaze falling upon a woman in her twenties. Her breasts were almost falling out of her top. Feeling a bit guilty, I turned my gaze away from the nubile woman. Instead, I watched a blonde surfer as he strutted toward the water, his board pinned beneath a muscular arm.

TOXIC

I felt a bit inadequate watching the hunk. I wasn't a slob, but I was far from fit. I hoped that Polly was as attracted to me as I was her, but sometimes I worried that I was letting myself go.

You need to spend more time at the gym. Or you could take up jogging!

Jogging could be nice. I could take a run through the suburbs early in the morning, come back, shower, and be ready for work before the sun came up! It'd take some effort, but maybe that's what I needed in my life.

Another scream rose up. Even Polly set her book aside and turned her head. The shout had been blood curdling.

"You heard that?" She asked.

"Yeah. Sounds like someone's having a good time." I joshed.

Both of us instinctively looked toward the water. Thankfully, Tucker was in sight. He was sitting on the edge of the shore, allowing himself to be battered by rippling waves. He held his arms up and flopped back against the water, as if he was on a rollercoaster.

"He's fine." I said aloud. I didn't know if I was reassuring my wife or myself.

"God." Polly said, glancing up and down the beach. "I wish people would calm down. There are families here."

The scream broke through the beach-chatter once again.

I stood and held a hand over my eyes, shading them from the sun. I looked for the screamer.

I saw him instantly.

He was walking out of the ocean, holding his face in his hands.

The flesh was melting off. It hung in thick strands between his fingers like fat dollops of molten mozzarella.

A small crowd of beachgoers had gathered around the shore, unsure what to do for the melting body as it stumbled up from the sea.

"Oh, God!" I heard Polly shout.

More people were noticing the horrific sight. The victim's screams were matched when several sunbathers spotted him.

I heard a woman shriek, a child cry, and a man shout:

"Get away from him!"

No one listened.

A surfer strode toward the melting man and held out his arms. Stupidly, I heard the surfer say:

"You okay, bro?"

The swimmer pulled his hands away from his dome. His face came away, connecting his skull to his palms in ropey strands. A spurting blurt of blood and gore tumbled from his lipless mouth and spattered across the sand. The surfer leapt back, retching, and crying.

I stepped off the blanket, still not sure I believed what I was seeing.

I was an office drone. I'd never seen a person die before... much less *melt*.

Melt...

TOXIC

The word swam through my head like a fattened trout in a shallow pond.

What was making this young man's face fall away from his skull? Had someone tossed a vial of acid onto him? I'd heard of such things before. I'd seen on TV that someone had been randomly assaulted by an acid flinging maniac in New York City last summer. They had been horribly disfigured for no reason.

I doubted that this poor bastard was going to just be disfigured. Whatever was melting him was eating through every layer of tissue it touched.

"Get back!" I heard a woman shout.

"Shit! Someone call 9-1-1!" A large man hooted.

"Oh, God!" Polly rasped. "Tucker! Tucker!"

I turned away from the sight a few yards away from us and spotted my son.

Tucker hadn't noticed the chaos occurring down the beach. He was floating on his back, and his ears were submerged in the ocean.

My only concern was to take my son away from the horror on the shore. I raced away from the blanket and dashed toward the water. I knifed through the sea's surface and scooped my boy up. Tucker yelped in surprise and clung tight to my arms.

"Don't look!" I shouted as I hoisted him up and buried him against my Hawaiian shirt. He squirmed and wriggled in my arms, upset by the sudden shift in attitude and my raised vocals. He probably thought I was mad at him, poor thing.

TOXIC

I sloshed through the water and made my way back toward the beach. I looked behind me in time to see that—

—there was something beneath the ocean's surface.

It was long, flat, and multicolored, and it was expanding like a stain.

More screams rose from all around me as the colors sifted through floating, swimming, and panicking bodies.

I glanced back toward the melting man. He was on his knees, and his skin had been almost totally corroded. Clumps of sludgy muscle slipped away from his bones, and piles of curdled blood plopped against the sand. His arms dangled from their sockets, sloughing skin and meat. The piles of soupy flesh surrounded him was like a yellowed garland.

I watched in terror as his head tilted down... then detached from his neck and landed with a moist *thud a*gainst the beach.

My brain scrabbled to understand what had happened. Two things were clear to me. despite the anxiety and terror racing through my blood and clutching my heart, I knew this:

There was *something* in the ocean.

Whatever it touched... *melted*.

Polly was standing by our blanket, holding her mouth with her hands. She had been screaming while I retrieved our son.

Meeting my wife, I deposited Tucker into her arms. I wasn't being a chauvinist; I just knew she wouldn't believe Tucker was safe until she was holding him herself.

Tucker was weeping. "Wh-what happened, Momma? What'd I d-do?"

"Oh, hon! I'm so thankful your safe!" Polly began to smother him with kisses and hugs.

I looked around the beach. People were running now. More melting bodies came stumbling drunkenly from the water. I watched as a large woman's breasts slid down her chest and slopped into the sand, laying like abandoned jellyfish on the shore.

I watched as a ten-year-old crawled out of the water. He was pulling himself with his hands. His body was cut open beneath the hips. A long trail of innards drifted back and forth in the waves behind him.

That could've been Tucker. I thought. *If I wasn't fast enough... Tucker would be melting too.*

The nebulous quilt beneath the water was impossibly large. It continued to stretch and expand, and it wore a layer of gore across its surface. I watched as dislocated organs bobbed like buoys on the ocean's rumbling top.

Whatever *it* was... it was huge. About thirty feet long.

Slowly, the insubstantial frame of the oozing creature broke through the water's surface and began to rise up toward the beach. It moved like an organic wave. Blood sluiced and splashed down its rippling frame. The ocean itself had turned vibrant red.

TOXIC

I could see an eyeball peering out beneath the fibrous curtains. The eye was the size of a beachball, and it was stained with crimson veins. Its pupil was a narrow reptilian slit.

Below the eye, there was a row of vents. Each one was rimmed with tender tendrils, which whisked back and forth along the sides of the vertical openings.

The monster rising up from the sea reminded me of an expanding umbrella.

The creature enveloped the edge of the beach, crawling away from the water and toward us with oily speed.

I turned and shouted at my wife and son: "He have to run!"

Polly stood, holding Tucker in her arms. She caught sight of the gelatinous mass swelling up from the ocean.

'Wh-what is it?" She asked, her tone incredulous.

We backed away from the thing together, both unsure whether what we were seeing was real or not. I was half convinced that I'd be awoken from this nightmare if I pinched my arm-flesh.

A thick tentacle flopped out from one of the vaginal slits along the creature's edge. The tentacle was black, oleaginous, and slick. It didn't have any suckered pads, like an octopus. It looked more like a cylindrical pipe, tipped with a hardened talon. They reminded me of scorpion stingers. It swam through the air and dipped toward us.

TOXIC

"Run!" I spun my wife around and we dashed away. I heard the tentacle *thump* onto the ground behind us.

Tourists were crying and screaming all around us. As we raced toward our resort, I watched as more tentacles sprang loose from the creature's multiple orifices.

Ahead of me, a surfer tripped on his own feet. A tentacle was quick to spear him through the back, pinning him to the sand. The writhing pipe lifted the surfer's flailing body into the air, then sucked him into the creature's maw. I saw a clear goo drape the surfer's body, searing the flesh away from his squirming bones.

It melts people. It melts them and sucks their sludge up. Fuck me, this is insane!

Tucker was crying, as if he'd scraped his knee. I wished we could slow down to comfort him, but all we could do was run.

A tentacle zipped over my head. I ducked down, holding my skull in my hands. I could hear bits of acidic goo dropping from the limb and sizzling against the sand. A dot of fluid hit my back, and my skin was instantly lit aflame.

Holy shit!

I scrambled forward, catching up to my wife and son.

Tucker was looking at the monster over his mother's head, his mouth agape.

He'll never sleep soundly after this. My thoughts were absurd, but that's what adrenaline does. It forces you to focus on things that ground you, rather than the unbelievable, swollen terror coming up from the sea.

What is it? An alien? A sea-monster? A government experiment unleashed upon the populace. Maybe it's a jellyfish mutated by toxic waste! Ha!

I circled around my family and struggled to slide the glass door open. Polly dived in—her arms tight around Tucker. As I stepped in, I was suddenly bumped hard by a crashing body. A blast of hot air escaped me as the hulking man forced his way into our room.

At first, I felt like throwing a punch at him. Then I saw that he was pulling a six-year-old girl behind him.

"I'm sorry! I'm sorry!" The man shouted.

I wavered on my feet, clenching my fists beside me. The man was a stranger, and I was uncomfortable with his presence even though he was obviously just trying to evade the same monster we were.

He pulled our door shut and closed the blinds. Then, he gathered up his sobbing child and held her close.

They were obviously related. With their short, blonde hair and dabbled green eyes, I could see she'd inherited many of his traits. The man was fat, dressed in trunks and a shirt eerily similar to mine, and his eyes were hidden behind an expensive set of sunglasses. His child was wearing a sunhat. I'm surprised it hadn't flown off as she was carried away from the ocean and toward our resort room.

"I'm sorry." The man said, glancing apprehensively from me to my wife. "I-I saw you guys go through here and just—I was just thinking about keeping Talia safe." He hefted up his daughter.

Outside, I heard someone scream. The noise was cut in half with a *splash*.

"I'm Roger." The man said.

"Jeff." I returned. "This is Polly, and Tucker."

'Did you see what happened?" Roger asked, biting his lower lip. "I mean... where did it come from?"

"I dunno. I've never—erm—seen anything like it." I eventually responded when the hesitancy surrounding us became cloying.

The ground shook beneath us.

I rushed over to my wife's side and took her free hand. Her other arm was looped around Tucker, pinning him to her body. Dismally, the boy looked toward me.

"D-does this mean we won't be goin' to Disney?" He asked.

I could've laughed. Maybe I needed to. Instead, I just ruffled his hair.

Roger walked over toward us, carrying Talia. The girl buried her face against the side of her father's neck, as if she was scared of us and not the creature outside.

The ground shook again. The painting hung between the beds unlatched from the wall and hit the ground. Polly yipped and clutched my hand tightly. Her fingers were like cactus barbs.

TOXIC

There were more screams rising from outside. I could hear metal grinding against metal as well. The creature had wormed its way up the beach and was now destroying the cars parked in the lot adjacent to the resort. Maybe, it would slither past the building and make its nasty way toward the city.

"I've never heard of anything like this." Roger said with a whimper. "You think it's like... a *Godzilla*?"

I felt my skin crawl. "It can't be. Something that big... someone would've seen it before today."

I recalled the snippets of horror I'd seen as I pulled Tucker from the sea. The creature had grown and expanded like a time-lapsed fungus. It had started small, and it had grown as it consumed the tourists and surfers around it. The more it ate, the bigger it got.

I didn't know that for certain. I was just working on loose theories. But it was all I had.

Rather than express these thoughts around the kids, I said:

"Hey, Roger, you have a car?"

Roger shook his head. "I... we called an Uber from our hotel to come to the beach today." He frowned. "My husband caught a bug on the plane so he's staying in today."

He might have gotten lucky. The sardonic lilt to my thoughts was becoming a permanent fixture. *He's probably snug in bed, not aware of the horrible thing that almost ate his husband and daughter!*

TOXIC

"Can I use your cellphone?" Roger asked Polly. "If you have one. I... I want to call him and let him know what happened."

"Sure." Polly said, sympathetically. For the first time since I'd handed our son to her, she released Tucker.

Then, she began to weep.

"What is it?"

"I left my cell in the beach bag." She admitted with a sniffle.

"I have mine." I said, stooping down and pulling my luggage bag out from beneath the bed. "Here." Handing the phone to Roger, he struggled to balance his daughter on one side before dialing, then pinning the phone between his head and shoulder.

We all waited with pregnant breath.

Sighing, Roger said, "Voicemail." His inflection changed. "Hey, hun. Please, call this number, okay? And be careful. Something... there was an attack at the beach. Talia and I are fine. We're hiding with a kind couple—uhm—I love you. Call me. Love you."

He handed my phone back.

"I didn't know what to say. I don't think I could describe it even if I wanted to."

The ground shook again. It felt like we were getting previews to an encroaching earthquake.

"Here. You can sit with us." Polly said, patting the side of the bed.

Roger came over and joined our family. His eyes were wet, and his lips were trembling. He was trying to be strong for his daughter, but he was crumbling. I was only a few feet from a breakdown myself.

I walked over to the blinds and parted them. Looking outside, the beach had been transformed into a hellscape. Greased lumps of flesh and discarded limbs were scattered through the sand. An oily patch of degloved skin lay askew on a half-sunken surfboard.

I could see a woman crawling amid the remains of the dissolved masses. Half of her face had been sheared away, exposing clumps of tattered tissue and wriggling musculature. The woman's left arm was dangling by a red strand. The right was totally gone.

She was walking on her knees. I could see a slippery tube wiggling its way out from the back of her bikini pants. Her bowels were trying to run away from her stomach.

The creature was nowhere to be seen. It had left a trail of mutilation behind it, and now it was gone.

Had it returned to the ocean? Or had it progressed into town to continue devouring innocent people?

"Hey, I'm Tucker." My son said.

I caught him shaking Talia's hand, offering her a warm smile. She wiped away a tear with the heel of her hand before whispering, "Hi."

I felt a swell of pride. My son was being polite to the terrified girl, putting his own tears aside. I wanted to tell him just how wonderful he was. Promises felt empty in these moments, but I wanted to tell him that we'd make it through this... because God wouldn't dare let such a sweet boy die.

We could all die. All of us. A sliding glass door isn't going to hold back... whatever that thing is.

"Maybe they're talking about it on the TV." Roger suggested.

"Good idea." I took the remote and turned on the tube. Huddled together, we watched live footage from a helicopter over the beach. There were bodies and pools of steaming goo scattered across the sand, crawling over the parking lot, and slicing through the buildings. The camera followed the trail until it met the source of the splatter.

Polly gasped.

Roger covered Talia's eyes and turned her head away from the screen.

"D-dad... what's happening?" Tucker asked.

"I don't... I don't know, son." I said.

On the screen, we could see the slithering mass of formless flesh making its way toward... an equally disgusting creature.

"There are two of them?" Roger asked.

"Look." I pointed. "One's bigger than the other."

Maybe it had more to eat on the other side of the city.

The two polyps slid toward each other, overturning cars and rumpling the buildings around them. Thick gullies of saucy fluid fell from their bodies and sprayed the streets. Through the grainy footage of the camera, I could see people being washed in acidic juice. They melted almost instantly, pouring together to form fleshy streamlets.

I couldn't believe it, but I was actually becoming *used* to the sight of a human body disintegrating. Still, a fresh batch of horror sparked through my chest when I imagined my son and my wife mixed up in the broth.

I tried to focus on the voices of the newscasters playing over the footage. They were just as shocked and disturbed as we were, but they maintained their tone to the best of their abilities.

"If you're just tuning in... this is not—uh—a hoax. This is not manipulated footage. This is live. Wh-what you are seeing is happening. Two... organisms have come out of the sea."

The newscaster paused. Her partner took over to continue the broadcast.

"They are now meeting in the middle of a city off the coast of Florida. We have yet to confirm what—uhm—exactly these things are."

"Yes, Steve. There's been speculation but no confirmation. As far as we know, there was no warning. These creatures appeared from the ocean and... and are now meeting. If you are in the area of... if you are in the city of Starmouth, Florida, then it's advised that you remain indoors and as far above ground level as possible. An acidic liquid is falling from the creatures which—yes—which is dangerous. I repeat, the creatures should not be approached, and the liquid they produce should not be—oh, God. I'm going to remind viewers once again that this is live footage, and it is—holy shit. I can't look."

On screen, we watched as a naked man ran out of his house and dived headfirst into the wave of fluid rippling around the edge of the bigger creature. He lay in the swampy mess, flopping like a fish pulled from water. His skin seemed to run away from his ribcage, exposing reddened bones.

The skeleton began to dissolve as well, breaking like dropped clay.

"Wh-why did he do that?" Roger asked.

"Maybe he didn't know it would hurt him." Polly theorized.

"No." I scratched the back of my head. "No. I think he... he knew. He had to have known."

Internally, I wondered if he didn't have the right idea. Get it over quick rather than wait it out.

Stupid. Don't think that way.

"Hey, Tucker, Talia, do you wanna play with coloring books?" Polly asked, kneeling by my luggage.

Tucker glanced at me, looking for approval. I gave it to him with a nod.

"Here. We've got *Star Wars*. Do you like *Star Wars*, Talia?" Polly held up the book and flipped through the pages. I wondered if she was looking for any big, melty monsters. If she found any, I'm sure she'd have pulled those pages out before the kids saw them. Deciding that the book was fine, she handed it to Tucker.

"We haven't shown her *Star Wars* yet." Roger said as his daughter sat down beside Tucker. "Phil keeps telling me we need to, but all she ever wants to watch is *Sing*."

"Heh." I smirked. "Tucker was addicted to the sequel."

Roger suddenly broke into a sob. Polly sat next to him and put her arm over his shoulder. Despite the fact that we didn't know this guy from Adam, she comforted him as if they were old friends.

"I just... I'm worried about Phil." He whispered so Talia couldn't hear. "He hasn't called you back yet, has he?"

I checked my phone. No missed calls.

I was a little let down myself. No one from home or from work had called to ensure the safety of me or my family. I had a few messages, but they didn't seem overly concerned.

"Nothing yet. Maybe he's sleeping through it all." I said, looking for the best outcome. I wanted to put a positive spin on everything that came our way.

"What are they doing?" Roger asked. "What's happening?"

I took in the television once more. The newscasters were still talking, but I couldn't hear them. I was fixated on the horror ahead.

The organic mountains of oozing flesh and writhing tentacles met. Their hulking forms collided like wet towels. Clumping together, the beasts formed one massive lump, which simmered and sputtered like frying meat. Zig-zag jet-streams of fluid were flung from the vents around the rims of the creature.

"It's like... cells." Roger said.

"What?" I asked.

"Sometimes, cells come together, you know? Blood-cells? Or... germs. They look like what you'd see in a microscope."

"It's huge now." Polly said. "I mean, the one we saw was already... what? Thirty feet?"

"God." I muttered.

"What if there are more?" Roger asked. "What if they keep combining and growing until..."

He didn't need to finish his statement. I imagined a multicolored, lumpy, grotesque sheet spreading all over Florida, and beyond. I imagined fields of people being melted into a gummy paste and swallowed up by the sucking vents along the monster's frills.

The scummy creature began to wriggle along the city. Buildings were pushed down and stamped beneath its leaking edges. I could see herds of people dashing away in terror.

The camera had no choice but to capture their final moments.

Tentacles whipped out and skewered bodies. I saw an explosion of gore as a man was stabbed through the back and lifted into the air. His arms and legs hung limp and his head tilted toward the sky. The tentacle writhed in the air, turning him upside down, then slammed him into the earth. A smear of blood followed as he was dragged into the nearest maw.

I saw more suicides too.

TOXIC

Some people imitated the man that had dived into the goo, while others leapt from their buildings right before the structures crumbled.

Behind it, the creature left a wake of gore and destruction.

"This is my favorite character." Tucker told Talia, showing her the coloring book. "He's called a 'Wookie'." I was thankful the kids were distracted. The events playing out on our hotel-room television were beyond ghastly.

"This just in," the newscaster's voice broke through my revere. "Another creature has been spotted off the coast. I repeat... another creature has been seen rising out of the ocean. As of yet, we still have no word on what these things are. The President has remained silent, as have the—"

The floor rumbled before the TV and the lights went off.

"Whoa. What happened?" Roger said.

"There was another one. Did you hear that?" Polly stood.

The floor shook once more.

I returned to the blinds and pried them apart. Looking out on the beach, I shouldn't have been surprised by what I saw.

But I was.

Three more creatures were coming up from the water, leaving slug-trails of oily poison behind them.

One was directed toward the resort. It would be upon us in no time.

Could we run?

I doubted it.

"What is it?" Polly asked.

Blinking away tears, I said: "Don't panic."

Polly and Roger's eyes both widened in their skull, but they calmed when I tilted my head toward the children.

Slowly, I stepped around the bed, stooped down, and examined the pages of the coloring book. "Hey, gang. You wanna go to Disney?"

Tucker and Talia looked up at me with flummoxed faces. They knew I was lying, but they also knew that they needed the lie as much as I did.

Roger helped Talia up, then he carried her in his arms.

I held Tucker. He clutched me tightly, digging his digits into my shoulder.

"What are we doing?" Polly asked.

"We're going to run." I said. "And whoever gets to Disney first... wins."

Roger swallowed loudly.

"Okay. Let's get ready... get set..."

I heard the glass crack and splinter behind us. Polly yelped. Tucker buried his face into my neck.

"Run!" Roger finished for me.

We stampeded toward the door. I had it thrown open quickly, and then we were in the hall. Racing down the lobby, I could hear a sloshing, ugly liquid fill our room. If we had remained even a second later, all of us would have been melted.

Again, my morbid mind wondered if that would have been for the best—

The walls behind us were warped. The massive organism was cleaving through the building. I could hear screams coming from other rooms as people were doused with the beast's fluids.

I saw a rush of liquid fill the floor behind us.

It streamed in, like the ocean into the Titanic.

We had to push hard to run down the length of the hallway and toward the lobby. I could hear Roger panting, Talia sobbing, and my wife shouting for God.

Roger described them as massive germ cells.

I now know what they are.

They're a cancer.

Earth has come down with a bad cancer, which is rapidly eating away at it.

They are living tumors.

We came into the lobby and raced toward the front doors. When we hit a wall of sunlight, Roger and I both slowed down and turned.

Standing in the parking lot, we watched as the sluggish tumor wormed its way through the other side of the building. It had cut a line right through the resort's center, like a knife through a crumbly pie.

A realization slammed into me.

Polly wasn't with us.

"What happened to her?" I screeched toward Roger.

Roger looked around, realizing what I meant.

"She was right behind me! I know she was!" He declared.

"Mama!" Tucker exclaimed, pointing toward the entrance of the resort.

The automatic doors skimmed open.

Polly walked out on unsteady feet.

I turned Tucker's head away with a moan.

Polly landed on her knees.

I watched as her flesh fell away from her face and landed in a swampy puddle around her. Her clothing came unwound, and her skin scuttled away from her bones. The liquid that had contaminated her was eating her as quickly as a starving animal ate ravaged roadkill.

I wanted to run to her, but I knew that if I touched her... I'd be melted by the corrosive material as well.

"Polly!" I shouted.

She cocked her head to the side. A piece of cheek meat flopped away from her skull and splattered against her shoulder.

Her mouth fell open and a rush of blood cascaded out. Crimson streams poured from multiple openings.

"Mama!" Tucker screamed into my ear. I held the back of his head in a firm hand, keeping him faced away from his mother as she fell to pieces.

"I didn't—oh, God. I didn't realize she'd fallen behind! Oh, God! I'm sorry! I'm so, so sorry!" Roger cried.

I couldn't respond. I just watched as Polly fell back and splattered across the ground in a greasy smear.

My wife was nothing more than a stain.

TOXIC

All of our love, all of our happiness, and the entirety of our future... was reduced to this. I wished I could scoop her remains up and rebuild her like a snowman.

My heart cracked in two and my knees slammed together.

No. No. No. She's not dead. She can't be dead. No.

"Hey." Roger jarred me away from my shock. I realized that I was clutching Tucker's skull so hard my knuckles had turned white.

"Hey, I'm sorry. But we have to go." Roger said. "We can't stay here."

I turned my eyes away from my wife's liquefied body and gave Roger a mournful expression.

"We have to go, man!" He said, once again.

"Where?" I muttered.

"I don't know. Anywhere but here!" Roger said. "We can't stay. We have to keep running until—"

I turned my head back to the ocean. More slobbering creatures were swelling up from the water. I could see them growing like flowers. They opened and expanded, making the first creature look like an infant.

They'd keep coming... and coming... and coming. They'd combine into one massive mountain of melting flesh and angry tentacles.

This is how it begins.

This is how it ends.

Slowly, I began to walk away from Roger and toward the beach. Tucker struggled in my arms.

"Where are we going, Dad?" He whispered. I could feel his heart pounding like a hammer on an anvil. "Why are we leaving without Mom?"

I sobbed. No answer I could give would be the right one.

"Hey! Hey, man! Come on! Come back!" Roger screamed as I made my way out of the lot and onto the beach. The sand stung, but I ignored the pain.

"Hey! You can't go out there!" Roger continued.

'Tucker! Tucker, come back!" Talia said, raising her little voice for the first time since we'd met.

Listen, I didn't want things to end this way. No one did. But I really didn't see any alternative. A life without Polly was no life worth living, and as selfish as it may have seemed... I didn't want Tucker to suffer through survival.

If we ran, we'd just have to run until there was nowhere left ahead or behind us. We'd live in fear, if we even lived that long.

I'd lived a good life, and so had he. Tucker had been loved, cared for, and allowed his fun. He didn't know what he'd be missing, and that was for the best.

Roger and Talia eventually stopped calling after us.

I took a curious glance behind me. The man and his daughter were gone.

I hoped they would make it, but I had my doubts.

Over the horizon behind us, the conglomeration of oozing polyps had grown into a literal mountain. It pulsed and throbbed like a dying heart.

There was a vortex of eyes climbing up its center. Each eyeball was the size of a wrecking ball, and they were rimmed with green pus wads.

The volcanic structure of the monster was topped with a giant, twisting tentacle. It rose into the air and curved into a question mark.

I heard a continuous stream of sobs rising up from the broken city. The entire populace was in lamentation. It was an apocalyptic image, straight out of the Bible and stamped over the sunny Floridian landscape.

This is how everything ends. I thought. It had become a mantra. *No one will survive. No one.*

I looked away from that horror and searched through the beach for our blanket. It was half-submerged in sand. Trampled by stampeding feet and crushing tentacles.

I stooped over and pulled the beach towel free. It was spattered with blood, but none of the body-melting goo had reached it. I sat Tucker down on the blanket and joined him by his side.

"Wh-what are we doing, dad?" Tucker asked.

I put an arm over his shoulder.

"Why aren't we running?" Tucker continued.

I wished I could answer, but my words were clogged in my throat.

"There's more. They're going to get us! Dad, w-we... you have to keep me safe. Y-you have to keep me safe!" He wrapped his arms around me and began to weep.

I held him close and watched as more organisms rose from the ocean and ambled toward us.

TOXIC

I'd promised my son a day at the beach, and that was exactly what he would get.

Maybe, the both of us would go into the ocean, and he could use me as a launch pad—

The Cum House

1

"We *always* had us a Cum House. Most folks had an outhouse, where they did all their shittin' and pissin', so we didn't think thar was nuthin' wrong with havin' us a place fer cummin'!"

The old man scratched his balls and hocked a spit wad into the tin cup he kept on the arm of his rocking chair.

Winnow had no idea what to say. The first thought that sprang to mind was: *we're definitely going to have to edit some of this out.*

Winnow and her camera crew were stationed on the porch. Paw-Paw Mortimer was sitting in his usual spot, rocking back and forth on a creaky wooden chair. His hound dog sat by his feet, fat and gassy.

The pooch farted and groaned in his sleep. The old dog reminded Winnow of a bean-bag; it was so rumpled.

"Anyhow," Paw-Paw continued. "That's where the haunt is. Figger it's cuz poor Grandpop Mortimer done passed away in the Cum House not even thirty years prior. Though, he's never haunted it 'fore now."

Paw-Paw snorted and hawked another gob of yellow phlegm into his tin can. The can was almost filled to the brim with gunky fluid. Paw-Paw appeared to be struggling over a bronchial cold. He coughed into the air, not bothering to cover his whiskered mouth.

If he gets me sick, Winnow thought, *I deserve a raise.*

Fuck.

I deserve a raise anyways.

Winnow was leading the team at *Ghost Challengers*. A new reality show sponsored by an up-and-coming streaming service. The show was half paranormal investigation, half contest. And so far, as an expert in the supernatural, Winnow was finding the whole concept pretty insulting.

Each episode, she and her opponents were sent out to a place where ghosts had been sighted. Whoever got the most convincing evidence—or outright proved it to be a hoax—won the challenge.

Winnow was a serious academic. Or... at least she liked to think she was. She had dedicated much of her young life to researching ghosts, hauntings, and demons.

She had been discovered by the producers of *Ghost Challengers* through her social media. She was offered a position in the show and had been flown out to their shabby studio on her own dime. She wondered if contestants usually had to buy their own airline ticket. She doubted it. But the reward was worth the spent money. The winnings included a book publishing deal and a grant for further research.

It was just what she needed.

What she *didn't* need was to be forced into petty squabbles between herself and the opposing ghost-hunters. She also hadn't expected to play so many inane trivia games in a closed set that was designed to look like a spooky old mansion.

And now... we're doing a gross-out. Fuck.

She was already embarrassed, and not a single episode of this tacky show had aired yet.

Winnow glanced toward the nearest camera. Sitting behind it, Herb gave her a frown. She and the cameraman had gotten close enough to consider themselves friends. She barely knew the other crew members scattered across the porch—but Herb was good people.

There was a sound engineer named Andrea, and another camera operator named Jorge. He was facing Paw-Paw Mortimer, capturing the old hillman in all his fetid glory.

Winnow had no clue where the producers had dug Mortimer up, but she was sure it was somewhere soggy and sweaty. He was a rail-rod thin mountain man, with a gnarled, yellowed beard, flaky skin, and lumps on his nose. He was wearing overalls, and his pits were coated in coarse hair. He smelled like a soiled diaper. Sitting near him, Winnow's eyes were watering.

The stipulation of the challenge meant that the contestants were only given a location pin on their phones. They had to figure out who was being haunted, and the nature of the spectral sightings themselves.

Following the location pin had brought Winnow and her team into the mountains two hours away from their studio. Driving through the forest in their van, Winnow had spoken with her crew:

"I don't think anyone lives out here." She flicked a lock of purple hair away from her brow with one hand while she adjusted her coke-bottle lenses with the other.

"Maybe we're supposed to camp." Andrea said.

"They really don't even tell y'all about the assignments, huh?" Winnow asked.

Jorge shrugged. "Nope. Don't want us influencing your search, I reckon."

They had pulled up to the house immediately after catching sight of it through the trees.

Max's van was parked in the side yard. Winnow felt her guts rumble when she spotted the vehicle.

Max was the main competition. He was smart, handsome, and funny. Which meant that he had become the show's hero.

Meanwhile, while Winnow was putting in equally hard work... she received less attention from the judges.

I'm an autistic ghosthunter with no friends. I didn't know it was going to be a popularity contest. They barely looked at the pictures I took from the Dobbsin house. Despite the crazy evidence I got there... they just scanned the pages and moved on to Max's.

Gritting her teeth, Winnow was quick out of the van.

Jorge and Herb got out with their cameras, and Andrea followed with her padded mic. They followed close behind Winnow. Max was nowhere to be seen, but Winnow caught sight of the old-timer sitting on the porch. They approached him quickly.

"Yer friends already said you'd be 'round." The man had said.

Knowing that he didn't need to hear any more about the structure of the show, Winnow asked him,

"Is this the haunted house?"

"Well, you better sit down fer a second, girlie. You and yours ought ta hear my story 'fore ya go snoopin' 'round here."

The old man was gnarled and nasty. His bare toes were topped with school-bus yellow nails. His skinny arms were draped with tenuous flesh. She saw that his fingers were so calloused, they were almost as white as paper. His beard was stained yellow around his mouth, and one of his eyes was gummy with an infection.

Swallowing through the stink, Winnow asked, "are there ghosts in this house?"

The old man spat into his cup. "Nope."

Winnow sighed. This man was a dead-end and a waste of time. She was about to tell her crew to pack up and get back in the van.

Then, the old man said, "tha ghost's out in the Cum House."

Winnow scrunched up her face. "The—excuse me—*what*?"

Jorge gave Winnow a concerned look. He wore it well on his slender face.

"Do you mind speaking up, sir?" Andrea said, indicating the mic. "You're not really hooked in."

"Yeah. Sure, toots." The man coughed wetly. "We'se got us a ghost in the Cum House out 'round the back."

"I'm sorry, sir." Winnow started.

"Need me ta speak louder? That's 'bout as loud as I go, what with my throat bein' so stuffed. Ya 'know?"

"No. No. I think your fine. I'm just... I'm confused." Winnow said. "Are you saying, 'Cum House'?"

"Yip." The man said, leaning over to scratch his sleeping hound dog. "We *always* had us a Cum House."

2

After telling them his name and a bit more about the Cum House in fractured English, Winnow asked for the old man to elaborate on the death of Grandpop Mortimer.

"Well, shit. The Cum House was his idear in the first place! See, Grandpop and Grandma—that's my mom and pa, don't let their titles confuse ya. They ain't had nuthin' but boys. And you know how boys get. They sees fit ta jizz over everything once they learn how ta play with their peter. And they don't

TOXIC

really got a care where it goes or what it winds up smellin' like. Well, Grandma was awful mad at us boys, cuz back in them days ya had to wash the beddin's by hand.

"I 'member it like it was yesterday. Me and my brothers was upstairs while she yelt and yelt at Grandpop. I 'member her sayin' 'Saul, you better have you a talkin' with them pups, 'er they's gonna drive me plum up tha chimney with all-a them crusty blankets!'

"O' course, Grandpop knew boys would be boys, so he said, 'what else you want, Me-maw? Fer me ta rope up the moon and bring it down fer ya?' Well, she really pitched a fit after that.

"So, we had us a family sit down, and Grandpop asked us boys if we'se could resist our natural urgings. A-course we made plenty o' promises, then we went right back to spermin' our sheets! Well, this went on a mite while. Grandma would get riled, Grandpop would try and talk us into keeping our hands off our peckers, and we'd nod and promise, then get right back to it not two or three nights later.

"So, that's why Grandpop decided we needed us a Cum House."

God. How'd the producers find this guy? Winnow thought with a frown.

'Well, the Cum House was about the best idear Grandpop Mortimer ever did have! We'd go out there, blow some wax, and we'd be tucked in fer bed every night by nine! No more spoiled sheets, and no more yucky smells! Grandma was happy, and so were we!

"Well, it became a fixture of the homestead. Like a washtub, or a closet. We ain't thought nuthin' much about it. 'Fore long, we'd all grown up and learned it was way nicer to put our peckers in ladies rather than hol' em in our hands. My brother, Frank, moved in with a girl 'cross the creek. Then, Anthony wound up bein' an ass-blastin' fairy. We don't talk to him no more. Anyways, I done met my beloved Lucinda, and she could take a dick like a beaver chomps on wood!" Paw-Paw hooted before smacking his knee with a calloused hand. "She died early. So'd the baby. Right shame. Lucinda? She was a peach. A real splittail on 'er that'd make ya cream on sight!"

Paw-Paw's vision went distant. Winnow waited patiently, knowing she'd win no favors if she interrupted his train of thought.

"Welp. Anyway, Grandma died off too. So, I moved back in to take care of Grandpop Mortimer while he was on his own. And I noticed... he'd been usin' the Cum House."

Jorge held back a snicker.

Paw-Paw raised a bushy brow. "Laugh now... but every man needs a lil relief. I bet you do it yerself!"

"S-sorry." Jorge's face went scarlet.

Huffing, Paw-Paw continued his tale. "Well, Grandpop was out at the Cum House longer than usual, and it were getting late. So's, I went out and knocked on the door. When I didn't get no answer, I paused a mite. I didn't wanna open the door and get a look at my pappy's tool. But I was worried he'd gotten hisself in a spot. So, I took the door, swung it open... and he plum dropped out. His pants was 'round his ankles and he was still sportin' a mean ol' woody! "

Paw-Paw paused to spit into his phlegm can.

"I was so startled; I didn't even realize he were dead 'til after I done yanked his britches back up. I had to touch his rod. Just ta tuck it into his drawers. I ain't no faggot, like my brother Anthony. Ain't proud of that, but it's a fact o' life. Way I sees it, ol' Grandpop got a bit too excited, and his heart done gave out. Bet it was the nut of his lifetime though!"

"And you've seen his ghost around the—er—Cum House ever since?" Winnow asked.

"Naw. That was thirty years ago now that Grandpop popped his last. I didn't see the ghost 'til a few months back."

Paw-Paw rubbed his beard and held his breath. Winnow waited, hoping he'd hurry up and tell her about the ghost of his Grandpop.

Weird that he calls his dad "Grandpop". Well... that's not the weirdest thing going on here. Winnow thought with a sardonic lilt.

"Yer pals are out there now but..." Paw-Paw Mortimer leaned forward. His lips shimmied up his teeth, exposing blackened gums. His halitosis blasted her like an elephant fart. "They ain't gonna see nuthin' yet. You gotta be cummin' ta see the ghost."

TOXIC

Paw-Paw Mortimer led them around the house and into the woods.

Winnow flinched when she saw Max and his camera crew standing in a circle beneath a creaky elm. Max glanced up and gave Winnow a polite smile.

She scowled involuntarily.

Hidden through the tree-line, Winnow could see a small wooden shack. It was about the size of a porta-potty. Its walls leaned in, and the roof was made of rusted sheet metal.

It's just an outhouse.

"Yep!" Paw-Paw snorted and blew a clump of green sludge out of his nose. A twine-like growth of mucus hung from his nostril and clung to the edge of his mustache. "That thar's the Cum House!"

"Hey, guys." Max strolled toward them. He was tall, sexy, and blonde. His hands were in the pockets of his tight jeans, and his eyes were hidden behind a pair of reflective sunglasses. "Crazy story, huh?"

"Never heard anything like it." Jorge said in a whisper.

"Come on now, ya'all!" Paw-Paw called out as he rustled through the trees.

The groups followed him.

By the time they reached Paw-Paw, he was pulling the door open and revealing the Cum House's insides.

The smell wafting from the building was abhorrent. It reminded Winnow of moldy Thai food. The ammonitic stench of dried sperm made her retch.

"Oh, it ain't that bad! Least fer us fellers, am I right?" Paw-Paw chirped with laughter, but the males in attendance were just as green-faced as the girls.

Winnow pushed her gorge down and peered into the receptacle. She hadn't known what to expect, but it wasn't *this*.

The Cum House had a foot of flat floor, then a "V" shaped trough, with a narrow slit at its bottom.

"You can jerk yerself over the trough," Paw-Paw explained, "and it catches it and dribbles it down ta a hole Grandpop dug. Jus' like a shitter!"

The idea sounded logical, but the execution was wanting. With no water to wash the slants, the walls of the trough were soaked in ancient jizm. Flaky, yellowed crusts had built up like cave-growths. And the line of the slit was congealed with sperm.

"Oh, Christ." Max put a hand over his mouth.

"Yeah. It does get a mite stinky. Well, what can I say, huh? It gets hot out in the summer!" Paw-Paw pulled at the straps of his overalls.

"Let's... uh... can you... can you tell us about the ghost?" Winnow asked.

"Yes. Tell us." Max cut in. "He told us everything about his father's passing but... said he'd tell the rest of the story when you guys showed up." He scratched the back of his head.

Good. We're on equal footing.

TOXIC

"Well, I didn't use the Cum House fer a bit after ol' Grandpop spent his last wad. In fact, I didn't feel like pulling my cord for quite a bit after that. Cuz every time I did, I pictured the feelin' of my Pappy's stiffy while I was tuckin' him back in his undies. But eventually, I got a *Sears* catalogue from town. And the tiddies in there just about blew my got-dang mind! I mean—out ta *here!*" He held his hands a foot away from his chest. "I couldn't put it off, ya know? Had to loosen some cock boogers! I had ta! So, I went out to the Cum House. It was real late at night—"

Mortimer raced from the porch out into the woods. He kept the image of the lady from the *Sears* catalogue in his mind. He couldn't afford to forget even a curve.

He thought—briefly—about his Grandpop as he swung the door open and stepped into the sweaty Cum House. The wood surrounding him was soggy, and the stench coming from the vent at the bottom of the trough was tangy.

Mortimer struggled to peel his pants away. He didn't wear briefs, but his cock was sweltered in sweat, which caused the fabric to cling to his skin. Pulling his pants down was like ripping Velcro. The brief spurt of pain didn't diminish his hard-on. In fact, it added a layer of sensitivity.

Gripping his penis in his hand, Mortimer began to pump.

Closing his eyes, Mortimer tilted his head toward the ceiling above him. He spied a clump of spider-eggs in the corner, where the sheet metal barely met wood. A spear of moonlight illuminated the cobwebs and landed on Mortimer's brow.

"Aw, fuck." Mortimer said. He was getting distracted, and his noodle was going limp. "Dagnabbit!" He squeezed his eyes and refocused his mind.

He pictured the model from the catalogue. A purty young thang with a heavy chest and a blue brassiere. Her knockers reminded Mortimer of Lucinda, back before she had died while giving birth to a sideways baby.

No! Don't go thinkin' 'bout that! Ain't nobody ever cum to the image of a woman's pelvis being cracked like a walnut cuz she tried to push a baby out tha wrong way! Well... nobody but a freak would cum to somethin' like that.

And Mortimer was no freak. His tastes were simple—even if not sophisticated. He liked titties, he liked ass, and he didn't mind a little bush dangling off a splittail.

Returning his mind to the model, he imagined pulling her bra off and slapping her fun-bags around. He watched them jiggle and dance on her chest. They reminded him of Jell-o bowls at a party! He yipped with joy as he battered the woman's breasts back and forth.

"Oh, sheee-yit! That's how I like 'em! All wiggly!" Paw-Paw Mortimer said.

"You like tha way they bounce?" He heard the model chirp in his ear. "How'd you like a taste?"

Would he ever!

He imagined her nipples like slabs of pepperoni. All areola, centered with prickly little buds for teats. He hoped they tasted spicy and sweet in his mouth.

"You can flick 'em, twist 'em, and tease 'em all you like, big boy! They's all yers!"

Paw-Paw Mortimer felt a rush of heat touch his crotch. He worked his free hand beneath his pelvis and cradled his saggy testicles. Thatches of overgrown hair stuck out in weedy tufts between his knuckles.

"Oh, boy! Imma blow you a cream-rocket that'll make ya scream!" He said.

He imagined the model lying back and holding the undersides of her titties in her hands. She smiled up at him, her lips wet and her eyes gleaming.

"Go on! Put it right 'tween these here hooters, Paw-Paw! Fill my valley!"

Mortimer was returned to the Cum House as an explosion of curdled jizz tore through his urethral pipe and blasted out from the end of his hose. His lumpy balls felt like hot coals in his hands, and he dropped them.

He looked down into the trough.

He almost leapt back and tripped over his drawers.

Floating in the center of the ventilated slants of wood... was the face of his Grandpop.

He saw the old man's visage as clear as day. It was pale and sickly, and his eyes were hollow sockets. His mouth was open... and it had collected all of the white ropes Mortimer had just blasted. Languidly, the old man sealed his mouth closed. He swished the jizz back and forth before swallowing it.

Grandpop opened his mouth, revealing a hollow hole. Not even a speck of man-batter stuck to his chapped lips.

The disconnected head released a gargled moan. It reminded Mortimer of a death rattle.

3

"Then what happened?" Max asked, enraptured by Paw-Paw Mortimer's disgusting tale.

"I hauled up my britches, then I done hauled ass outta thar!" Mortimer said. "After a while, I assumed I was seein' thangs. So, I went out and tried to baste my pecker again. Same results. Ol' Grandpop was there to lick all the nut I done wasted."

"Did he ever... abuse you as a child?" Winnow found herself asking. Perhaps it was a rude question, but Paw-Paw Mortimer had been nothing but frank so far.

"Nah. Licked my hide pretty durn good a time 'r two but... that's just the way ya reared a child back in them days. Never took no interest in sucking or fuckin' me if that's what you're getting at. No, I don't think he likes much being trapped in the Cum House trough. I think since he died, that's just where he turnt up. And now he ain't got no choice but to look on while his son... tends ta his needs."

'You... you still use the Cum House?" Max quarried.

"Not no more. Nope. Not since ol' Grandpop took to hauntin' it."

"Have you tried talking to him?" Winnow cut in before Max could ask another question.

"The only time I ever seent him... is when I'm cummin'. I think, since that's how he died, repeating the action works as a kind of... er... summoning. I went in thar and tried calling him up a time 'r two. I even brought in one-a them 'wee-gee' boards... but he don't show up 'les yer blowin' a load!"

Paw-Paw sighed, signifying the end of his tale.

"Now, yer producers said you'd be out here fer the night. Tha's okay by me. Jus' don't make too much of a ruckus when ol' Grandpop spooks ya! I's gotta get my beauty sleep, ya know?"

Winnow swallowed. "Wait."

Paw-Paw Mortimer met her eyes. His optic bulbs were crusty and sallow. Even looking at them filled her throat with bile. She held back her revulsion to push out her question: "Does it work for women?"

"Whaddya mean?"

"Do you... gotta be putting sperm into the trough to summon him or... does it work for women to?"

Paw-Paw shrugged. "T'aint had no girls out here ta try it out!"

The old hillbilly turned and waddled back toward his house, leaving the ghost hunters in stunned silence.

TOXIC

4

While the camera and sound crew set up their respective equipment around the Cum House, Winnow and Max walked to Winnow's van for a breather. She didn't like being nearby her competitor, but after the story she had just heard... she needed to keep a foot in reality. She felt Max's presence would help.

"Hey." Max said as Winnow rolled the door of her van open and sat down on the floor. She dangled her feet out of the vehicle and gazed toward the house through her glasses.

"What's up?" Winnow didn't bother looking at Max's face. Her eyes were trained on the front porch. Paw-Paw and his bloated dog were sitting still.

"You really gonna try the... the House out?" Max asked.

"Aren't you?"

Max shook his head. "I don't think so. No."

Winnow saw an advantage in the competition. "Why not?"

"Well, it's disgusting, isn't it?"

"What? Cumming?"

His face went scarlet. Winnow had been paying attention to Max during their weeks against each other. Max was a sexless Baptist who took to ghost hunting because he felt it would prove the existence of the supernatural to nonbelievers. He was a hottie, but he was also driven by moralistic convictions. Masturbating on camera would be a no-go for him.

Has he ever masturbated? Winnow thought. *Of course, he does. Everyone does.*

Winnow tried to picture it.

"I dunno. This just feels weird. I don't know if Paw-Paw told the producers exactly what was going on, you know? Like, you remember that bed and breakfast from New Hampshire we flew out to last week?"

"Yeah." Winnow said, without commitment.

She really couldn't think of Max as anything beyond competition.

"And we didn't see anything? The best picture I got was of a fuzzy orb. Could've just been dust on the lens. But Chad told me that the owners sold their own building as 'the most haunted house in America'. They said we'd be guaranteed a sighting." Max said. "But I think they just wanted to be on TV."

"Hmm." Winnow sighed. 'Do you think that's what Mortimer wants? Five seconds of fame?"

"Maybe."

"You'd think he'd dress up if that were the case." Winnow chuckled.

Max sneered. "God. And the smell on him?"

The two laughed.

Max turned and sat beside Winnow.

"Who do you think will win?" He asked.

"I dunno." Her face fell.

She and Max had been assigned to the Cum House. She had no idea where Chad and Lucy were.

TOXIC

They were probably hanging out at a luxury haunted resort, or another bed and breakfast.

Lucky bastards.

"You've got a shot." Max said. "You just gotta... get out of your shell a bit. You know?"

Winnow felt her eyes roll in her skull. He was right. She wasn't playing for the cameras, and she wasn't mooching to the judges. All her footage was jargon, and all of her interactions were without humor. The audience wouldn't be rooting for her. Not while Max was charming the judges, Chad was milking his sob stories, and Lucy was as hot as a centerfold. Winnow vanished into the crowd wherever she went.

But, if there was even a shred of truth to Paw-Paw Mortimer's story... then Winnow was going to have to try it out. If anything, it would pull eyes toward her.

She imagined the comments.

Can you believe what Winnow did in the last episode?

She's crazy!

I bet that place smelled like ass! How'd she stand it?

She must be a freak!

Winnow wasn't sure if it would be "good" attention, but it was attention, nonetheless. And if she needed her research money, she needed to follow Max's advice and make an impression.

Maybe, I could be the Jackass *of ghost hunting. I could do something gross or dangerous in each episode building up to the finale. Ha!*

Winnow wondered if she was going crazy. She'd spent so much time crawling through dusty attics and dark hallways. Being a ghost hunter, eccentricity was just part of the job.

I need to be a little crazy to make this work.

5

"Is she really going to... try it?" She heard Jorge whisper to Andrea.

"You sure about this?" Herb asked as he helped set a Go-Pro camera onto Winnow's head. He put his fingers against her chin and tilted her face up. Winnow looked into the night's sky above them. The moon was like a white spotlight. It was beautiful out in the hills. Without the city's smog, Winnow could see through the sky and into the cosmos. The sky looked oily and glittery all at once.

She nodded.

"Just, be careful. I mean... we can blur out any nudity but... just keep your face up until... until you need to look into the trough." Herb stuttered.

"What, you don't think the people wanna see my downstairs?" Winnow joked.

"No comment, sweetie." Herb returned with a smile. He stepped back. "Okay. You are mic-ed, and you've got night vision video. Just... just be vocal about what's going on... but don't be obscene. If you want to make this count then don't give the producers a reason to censor us. Cool?"

Winnow nodded. She suddenly felt a surge of respect for sex workers and cam girls.

TOXIC

From the side yard, Max and his crew watched on with crossed arms. Max had reaffirmed that he wouldn't be entering the Cum House. Winnow felt—for once—like a stronger force than her fellow contestant. Max's cameraman was filming from a distance. Winnow could see that her competitor was speaking conspiratorially into the cameraman's ear.

Guess I'll learn what he has to say when this shit airs. Maybe some puritanical bullshit about how sin opens us up to the devil's influence.

He'd said such things before. Max was known for his catchphrase: "We're hunting ghosts... not demons!"

Winnow wasn't religious, despite the presumed "divine" nature of her work. She considered herself more of a "metaphysic enthusiast" than a "spiritual person".

If there was a God, would he put a dead man's face in the trough of a sperm shack?

Jorge stood ahead of Winnow, holding his camera up toward her face.

"Okay. Okay." Winnow muttered. "Y'all ready?"

"Ready on sound." Andrea confirmed, cupping a hand over her headphones.

"Cool. Jorge, call it."

Jorge gulped. "Aaaand... action."

Winnow tried to turn on the charisma, but she felt stilted. She walked toward the camera, addressing it as if the audience was sitting inside of it.

TOXIC

"After listening to Paw-Paw Mortimer's story, I've decided to test it myself. Yes, you heard me right. I'm going to see if the ghost of his father—Grandpop Mortimer—is truly haunting... the Cum House."

She heard Jorge stifle a giggle.

Easy edit. No need to retake the shot.

"She goin' in the Cum House?"

Winnow leapt around, startled to see Paw-Paw standing with his hands in the pockets of his overalls beside the house. Apparently, he had snuck up on Max and his crew as well. Winnow watched as they peeled away from him.

"Y-yeah." Winnow said. "I'm going in."

Paw-Paw smiled. In the moonlight, his yellow teeth seemed to glow.

"Good. I was hopin' you would." Paw-Paw walked away from the scene, circling around the front of the house and vanishing from sight.

Jorge turned the camera back to Winnow and gave her a slight shrug.

I was hopin' you would. Paw-Paw Mortimer's words trickled through her brain like a worm in a gutter.

She shuddered.

Winnow finally considered the impossibility of her encroaching task. When she masturbated at home, she usually lit a candle, drew a bath... or used her vibrator beneath her bedsheets. How could she expect to make herself cum in a shanty that smelled like dried spunk?

You could back out.

TOXIC

You could step back and cut the whole thing. Your crew would understand.

No. She had to do it.

Winnow moved toward the Cum House. Jorge stayed rooted in the spot, pivoting to capture her trek into the woods. She pulled the door to the Cum House open with a grunt. She was instantly hit with the sweltering stench of stagnant sperm.

Holding back a gut-churning cough, Winnow stepped into the shack. She drew the door closed behind her, sealing herself inside.

A sheet of moonlight poured in through the damaged roof, illuminating the sparkly base of the trough.

Don't think about it. Don't think about it.

Winnow pinched her eyes closed and pointed her Go-Pro toward the ceiling.

You don't have to think about it.

Just... do it.

She unzipped her trousers and pulled them down to her lower thighs. She didn't care about any of her vaginal drippings staining her pants. She wanted to be as clothed as possible.

She peeled her panties to the side, allowing her pussy to flex freely. Quickly, she dug a hand into her crotch and began to roll her digits.

Nothing happened.

She was too offended by the smells around her to focus on her fingering.

Clear your mind. Be a Jedi. Clear your mind.

She did.

Quite suddenly, she felt herself ease away from her surroundings. Winnow sifted through the woods, as if she herself had become a ghost.

Good.

Keep at it.

Just pretend your outside.

The summer air is hot and sweaty, but your pussy is out, and no one is going to stop you from playing with it.

Just breathe, honey. Breathe.

Strong sexual fantasies might come easy here. Remember how Mortimer described his visions of the model from the catalogue? Almost like a hallucination Or, like... a real encounter. Not that any woman in her right mind would want to fuck Paw-Paw Mortimer.

Don't think about him. That'll kill your buzz. Just ride it.

Ride it...

She was in a meadow now. Her hand worked her clit between her knuckles. Buzzing bees filled her stomach. Her eyes started to swim.

There was someone in the meadow with her. A tall figure with a sturdy frame and chiseled muscles.

Oh, God. Oh... Jesus!

The subject of her adolescent lust stepped into the moonlight. Naked, pulsating, and slicked with salty sweat. He smiled, and she felt her heart tremor.

It was her father.

Her first crush.

"Hey, hon." Her dad said. "Wanna see how proud I am of you?"

"D-dad?" She asked, struggling to believe what she was seeing.

Her father held out a hand. His other fist clutched the shaft of his throbbing sex.

6

After what felt like hours of ecstatic fucking, Winnow was thrown back into her body just as her orgasm broke. She felt an explosion of moisture between her fingers, drenching her hammocking trousers and trickling down her thighs.

Had no idea I was a squirter!

She leaned back, dinging her head against the sealed door behind her. A jet stream of fluid spattered against the trough.

Oh, fuck!

Immediately, she felt awash with shame. As always, her fantasies about her long-perished father were secrets she'd rather have kept to herself. Even then, she didn't partake unless she was simply allowing her mind to wander.

Would any of that show up on the Go-Pro? Jesus. I hope not. I don't think it would. That was all in my head, wasn't it?

It hadn't felt like a dream. She could still feel her father's hands on her breasts and his cock sliding into her—

She was back in the meadow, on her hands and knees. She could feel herself being filled... emptied... filled...

Oh, Daddy. I always loved you.

She was dismayed and ashamed by her incestuous fantasies. She remembered, as a young girl, thinking that she was "broken" for feeling this way toward her dad.

In therapy, she'd parsed through her fantasies, and concluded that she had wanted to replace her mother, since the woman had abandoned her as a child.

Now that she'd hallucinated a fuck-fest with her father... this symbolic explanation felt terse. In fact, it was downright stale.

Filled... emptied... filled...

It really had felt like a real experience. Even now, her vaginal tunnel was chaffed from friction. She could even feel his semen slithering inside her. Wormy, cold, and icky—

She hoped she wasn't airing her dirty laundry out for her camera crew and producers to see, much less the audience.

Oh, God. Winnow. What the fuck are you doing? You literally just jerked off on camera and... and you hallucinated about fucking your dad? What the fuck is wrong with you—

She turned her head down with shame.

She realized, as she looked into the trough, that she had totally forgotten *why* she'd stepped into the Cum House in the first place.

TOXIC

But, upon seeing the empty crevice, spattered with her juices and the curdled remains of Mortimer's seed... she realized that she'd done this for nothing.

There were no ghosts in the Cum House.

Winnow pulled her panties back over her juicy slit with a sigh and a sniffle.

After zipping up her pants, she pushed the door open and stepped outside.

We should cut the whole thing.

I'll threaten to sue if they air any of it.

God. I'm so ashamed. I can't believe I did this—

She saw Jorge lying on the ground ahead of her. His head had been broken open like a dropped cantaloupe. His brains sparkled in the moonlight.

Next to him, Andrea lay. Her neck had been blasted open. Frayed tissue hung out in clumpy roots. Her jaw was shattered through the middle. Blood flooded the dewy ground beneath her.

Winnow looked up, shocked and aghast.

She watched as Herb ran toward the van.

"Herb!" She shouted. "Herb! Wait!"

Herb turned his head but continued running. His face was knit with panic.

An explosion of gunfire cracked through the night.

Herb dropped. A hole blew through his chest and out of his back. It was followed by a flash of red blood.

Winnow covered her mouth, not caring that her hands were laced with genital grease. She stepped back into the Cum House.

She grabbed the door and slammed it shut.

Aside from the moonlight, she was surrounded by darkness.

What had happened?

She tried to remember if the sound of gunfire had broken through her dreams. Her visions had been so realistic, she doubted that anything could have stolen her away from it.

Because they weren't fantasies. They couldn't be. They felt like memories.

Winnow had actually *been* in the meadow...

...with her dad...

Holy shit. What the fuck is going on?

She heard a guttural blast.

Max screamed girlishly.

A thundercrack of gunfire caused Winnow's heart to flip.

She heard a wet explosion.

Another gunshot.

Another blast of wetness.

Max groaned. "P-please... stop. I... I... I didn't do anything to you. P-please..." Max pleaded through a mouthful of blood. "Pl-please, don't h-hu-hurt me!"

The gun roared again. Max's scream was cut in half with a violent *splash*.

The competition had literally been killed.

Winnow heard a van kick to life.

It squelched through the lawn, kicking up grass and dirt.

She heard the gunshot puncture the windshield.

TOXIC

The van crunched against a tree. Winnow heard steam escape the crumbled engine.

A door swung open. She could hear someone garbling for help. Their voice was split and soaked with blood. Hidden in the Cum House, Winnow had no choice but to listen as the shooter whistled his way toward the open door.

"H-help. Please." The injured victim mewled.

Winnow heard the shooter reload his rifle. He was quick and steady.

"HELP!" Max's female audio engineer screeched.

The gun replied with a booming cough. Winnow envisioned the woman's head popping like a water balloon. She pictured fingers of blood skittering across the dashboard.

The victim slumped onto the horn, causing it to bleat angrily.

God. God. Please. Please, God.

Her crew was dead, and so was Max's.

Everyone was dead, except for her.

And the shooter.

"Sheee-yit! Didn't realize thar'd be so many!" Paw-Paw Mortimer called out as he stamped across the backyard and ambled toward the Cum House. "Jesus, you city folk die *easy*!"

She could hear a shell fly out of a rifle.

"They didn't even *try* ta hide! Fuckin' idiots! Heh. I mean, I get they was yer friends but... Jesus-fuck, girlie! They was *smooth* in the head, weren't they?"

Winnow clutched her mouth. She pinched her eyes closed, squeezing loose fresh tears.

"I didn't wanna kill ya, girl. Ain't really had no other option. I hope you recognize that. You wanna open up that door and talk ta me face-ta-face?"

She shook her head, even though she knew he couldn't see her.

"Welp. That's fine. We can do it like this then"

A bullet smashed through the plank door.

It smacked into Winnow's head. A spark flew into the air as the go-pro shattered. Then, her brains spewed out behind her head and slipped into the trough.

7

Paw-Paw Mortimer pulled the girl-corpse out of the Cum House. She left a crimson carpet of blood behind her.

After he'd lined the cadavers up, Paw-Paw Mortimer went back to the Cum House and surveyed the damage. He didn't mind the blood stink, but he'd have to fix up a new door to replace the one he'd shot.

He stepped into the shack, closed the door, and dropped his pants.

Paw-Paw Mortimer's hands were slicked with blood, which helped lube up his swollen cock. He bit his lower lip and stared into the trough as he jerked himself off. His erection came fast, as did his fantasies.

C'mon. C'mon. C'mon. Paw-Paw Mortimer thought.

A milky explosion fell out of his crank and dribbled down his hand. Mixing with the blood, the sperm looked like a melted candy cane.

Paw-Paw Mortimer smiled as his seed spilled out from his fist and into the trough.

He could see Winnow's face, hovering inside the slants of wood. Her empty eyes stared at him bleakly, and her mouth hung open.

Paw-Paw Mortimer smiled. His theory had been proven correct.

Now that someone else had died inside the Cum House... he doubted he'd ever see Grandpop again.

Sure, he could've jerked off inside his bedroom, but Grandma Mortimer's ghost could get *awful* mad when he left stains on his blankies. Besides, he had gotten *used* to the Cum House, and he didn't like abandoning it.

According to the Mortimer family... every household in America needed to have a receptacle fer cummin'. Just like they had them a place fer shittin', pissin', and even spittin'!

"I can't tell ya how long I's been waitin' ta bust me a good nut in this here Cum House, girlie." Paw-Paw Mortimer said as he squeezed the last dribble out. "I jus' couldn't bring myself ta do it while ol' Grandpop was hauntin' this here place. But that's why I fixed this all up! I'd much rather see *yer* purty face than *his* ugly one!"

He watched as Winnow's ghost closed her mouth... and swallowed his load.

Anti-VaXXX

Just when I thought I had seen it all, I stumbled into the *Anti-VaXXX* club.

It was located in the rear end on an alley, positioned between a seedy hotel and a porno-shop. The nightclub's sign was unassuming. A small neon arrow pointed to a rust-stained door, which opened up to reveal a steep set of gross stairs. The steps were each encrusted with foul junk. Rainwater, mud, animal feces, used condoms, and even dirty needles. Walking into the club was a safety hazard. But that was all part of the thrill.

Once you descended the stairs and pushed through a curtain of plastic red beads, you would find yourself in a dingy room that smelled like smoke, stale meat, and ammonia. The room was small. Most clubs in our city had space for a stage, a bar, and enough spots for private and public lap dances. But not *Anti-VaXXX*. There was only a row of moist theater seats and a wooden platform which served as a stage. I didn't see any other patrons. Only a muscled bouncer with a veiny, bald head... and the girl.

TOXIC

The girl on the platform-stage reminded me of the Holocaust.

She was dangerously thin. Her bones seemed to be fighting to escape her flesh. Her cheeks and eyes were hollow, and her lips were a gray slit. She didn't wear any makeup, and her hair was greasy and unwashed. She swayed lethargically on stage, naked except for pasties and a G-String.

She was an ugly whore but... it wasn't about looks.

We weren't here to see her tits.

We were here to see her *disease*.

Rick had gotten us an invitation to the club after trolling through some online fetish forums. It was how he and I had met in the first place. We both had a strange affliction, which we had given up on justifying.

We were sexually attracted to diseases.

I honestly wish I could tell you how it started. Even in High School, I'd get hard if I saw a snotty nose, heard a harsh sneeze, or listened to someone complain about food poisoning. I liked to think it was about "control". Or, more importantly, the lack of "control". When people get sick, they are no longer the masters of their bodies. They are merely entities in a shell. A shell that expels hot waste and struggles to perform basic functions. A shell which must be attended to. A shell that releases the most ethereal sounds when disrupted.

Again, I wish I could explain it better... but my internet history speaks for itself:

Girl with stomachache shits pants in public.

TOXIC

Snot-suckers.
Girl gets fucked while in hospital bed.
Cancer screenings.
AIDS patient / Deathbed fuck.
Ill girls.
Regurgitation porn.
Recent amputee gets drilled.
And that only scratches the surface.

My fetish plunges deeper into dark territories. I've found videos of tumor-play, infection prodding, and even nostril fucking. Mucus, diarrhea, and vomit are all on my table.

I was open about my interests on several chat rooms, which were dedicated to illness fetishism. A lot of the people who attended those chats were curious passerby's, or outright clowns. You could always tell who was taking it seriously though.

Anyways, that's where I met Rick.

It was honestly like meeting my soul-mate.

Rick and I had our first meet up after two months of conversation in a porn-site chat room. We met in person because he wanted me to fuck his headache. I did as he commanded, lathering my cock against the roof of his mouth, trying to drive it up into his already scrambled brain.

Every time he had a migraine—and Rick had a lot of them—he'd call me.

I'm not really gay. At least, I don't think I am. I'm not straight, or bi, or pan, or ace... or anything. It's not the genitals that attract me to any specific partner... unless they're covered in warts.

TOXIC

I've been cultivating a farm of STDs in my crotch for a few years, and it's a playground Rick has loved to explore. When he works my pipe, my jizz comes out green, chunky, and it smells like curdled milk. He loves it when I stain his face and lips with my rot.

Rick's mouth is riddled with cold sores. Sores I gave him.

"Have you heard of *Anti-VaXXX?*" Rick asked me over breakfast after a night of fucking.

"Like, the folks that don't believe in vaccinating their kids?"

"No. Sorry. The club." Rick took a bite of cereal and chewed lazily. As the flakes turned to mush in his mouth, he watched me closely. "Have you heard of the club, *Anti-VaXXX?*"

"Nope." I said. I ran a hand through my gnarled hair. We were staying at Rick's place, and both of our bruised bodies were totally uncovered. I looked at the ingrown hairs spurting between his flabby breasts. I wondered how warm his pus would feel on my tongue, or if the infected deposits were no longer creamy... and would instead pop out like chunky cones.

Both of us were overweight. Our hope was to degenerate as we grew. We were flabs of flesh with endless potential. Every square inch of our bodies was an ailment waiting to be bred.

Rick thumbed through his newspaper, knowing all too well when my eyes were investigating him. He smiled out of the corner of his mouth and continued to talk. "It's a club I just read about on the forum. Apparently, they hire diseased girls."

"Yeah? Diseased girls, huh?" My curiosity was tugged. "Like, what type of—?"

"Death's door, man." Rick salaciously stated. "They hire them out of crack houses. Give them jobs no one else will. They see it as a charity thing. You know? Someone's gotta take care of their kids after they croak."

"So, it's basically a club... for *us*?"

"Sores, spots, and snot." Rick crossed his fingers over his pimply tits.

We went to the club that very same night.

And the girl in front of us looked as advertised.

She danced lithely on the stage, two-stepping and shaking her flat ass to a rap song that was playing over some crackly speakers. The lyrics were indecipherable. She looked as if she had never known the definition of the word "erotic", and that was fine with us. We didn't care if she was a good stripper. We just wanted to see her mold.

I was transfixed, and I barely noticed that Rick had waddled over to the muscled bouncer and started to whisper to him. In only a second, Rick and I were being led away from the musty theater seats and toward another door. This one was wooden and splintered. A crease ran through its center, and I could see lights flickering in the next room.

"Where are we going?" I asked Rick.

"You'll see." He smiled at me.

TOXIC

"Nice to meet you, by the way." The bouncer reached out and took my hand. His grip was wet, and his fingernails were long and yellowed. I held onto him for as long as I could without being impolite. I told him my name and he told me his was Takashi.

"Money's no object, Tak." Rick said, which shocked me a little. It was for me, but I lived in filth and squalor. Rick had a real job outside of his disturbed fetish. Although, he had never let slip where exactly he worked. This was my first indication that it was something big and important.

"I just want to show my friend here a good time." Rick said to Takeshi with a conspiratorial lilt.

Had Rick been here before? It seemed like it, even though he'd acted like he'd just learned about *Anti-VaXXX* this morning.

Maybe Rick took *all* of his sick friends to his favorite spot, eventually.

I felt pleased. I must have made a good impression. I found myself wishing I knew more about Rick. All I really knew was his body... and there were no secrets between us in that department.

Then again, when would we have had time to talk about our everyday lives? You can't really ask someone if they had a good relationship with their parents or if they've got a pet while they're pissing blood into a funnel stuck up your rectum.

One at a time, we stepped through the wooden door. I tried to casually look over my shoulder toward the dancing woman. She moved as if in a trance, performing for the empty room. I saw that her eyes were moon-white, and yellow deposits had clustered around their rims. Whatever infection she had; it had blinded her.

The next room was cold and white. A single lightbulb swung back and forth over our heads, flickering as it went. The area reminded me of a haunted house, or of a murderer's lair. I felt a prickle of unease crawl like a spider across my back. This only fueled my excitement.

"We've got a special treat for you today, Rick." Takashi clapped my friend between his heavy shoulder blades. "You both are going to have the time of your life. Come on." He led us toward the back of the cold room and pressed his fingers into the wall. With a load roar, he triggered a hidden switch which swung open an invisible door.

We're going to see something illegal. My heart swelled up like a balloon. I felt my teeth chatter.

We had to stoop down to fit through the narrow door. I could feel the frame biting into my fatty sides. With a grunt, I pushed myself through and found myself surrounded by darkness. Behind me, the door slammed shut.

"Takashi?" I asked.

"He's not here." Rick stated. "He doesn't come through with us." I felt Rick's hand encompass mine. "C'mon. Have a seat. Anywhere."

I squatted down and touched the ground. It was concrete, but a plastic tarp had been laid down. Crisscross-apple-sauce, I took a seat right where I was standing. With a lot of effort, Rick joined me by my side.

There was no hesitation, he reached between my legs and nudged my clothed penis with his sausage-y fingers. He had to lift my belly up to access my member, which had been stiff ever since we saw the sickly dancer.

My zipper pressed against one of my many warts and a delightful ache threaded through my body. I had to say something. "You've been here before?"

"Yes. A few times." Rick laughed. "I really think you'll like it."

"I already do." I admitted.

The lights came on abruptly.

We weren't alone.

Sitting in the opposite side of the room, there was a small woman with silky black hair and round cheeks. She was totally naked. Her breasts were flat, and her pubic hair was unruly. I felt my erection grow even stronger at the sight of her, and not because of her nakedness.

She was sick. Her skin was green and gray and so shallow you could see the network of veins knitting beneath her. Her belly was bloated, and my first thought was that she was pregnant. But I was quick to realize that it was filled with something else.

"Hello?" I offered after some silence crossed between us.

The sound of her stomach roiling was as load as a cannon's fire. She put her hands against her belly and her eyes conveyed panic. Her guts seemed to be churning, as if they were filled with maggots and rats.

"Get your pants off." Rick commanded.

I wrestled with my zipper and managed to pull my drawers down past my thighs.

When I looked back up, the girl was stamping toward me, holding her upset stomach with one hand and her mouth with the other.

"Oh, God!" I proclaimed.

She vomited on my naked cock. It rained out in a splattering wave of hot bile and chunky, half-digested dinner. The *glopping* sound of her gastric contents rushing up her throat and out of her mouth was music to my ears.

She fell down to her knees and directed her beige stream directly between my flexing thighs. I reached down and massaged my cock, grabbing up handfuls of her waste and using it as lube.

Rick was pulling his own pants off and struggling to his feet. I couldn't watch him. I was distracted by the mucus trails leaving her nose as she tried to hold in another rush of fecal-smelling stomach fluid.

Rick positioned himself behind her and gripped her hips. She vomited as he plunged in, coating my front in her slimy expulsions.

I felt my thumb catch a chunk of meat loosened from her oral cavity. I pressed it into the slit of my cockhead, plugging it up with her refuse as I cranked my shaft.

The orgasm I experienced was unlike any other. I could feel my semen spray up around the meat-

TOXIC

stopper I had pushed into my urethra. My hand squeezed out my load, forcing it up and toward her spewing face. Of course, my money-shot couldn't reach her. It simply plopped out of my cock and trickled down my warty shaft. But it's the thought that counts, isn't it?

Afterwards, she was empty, and so were we. We watched her crawl away from us, drained in more ways than one. Her legs seemed useless beneath her, and she crawled away on her hands. For the first time since we had met her, she spoke:

"I'm done. Please, let me be done."

I watched the creamy-green mixture of Rick's semen, and her anal juices pour out between her quavering buttocks. It left a trail behind her. It was like watching a snail move away from a pile of salt.

I stood up, tucking my penis and my belly into my soiled pants. My clothes were ruined. So were Rick's. But I couldn't spare a thought toward what our walk home was going to be like. I could only think about the amazing and grotesque experience we had both shared.

"The show isn't over yet." Rick said and pointed toward the woman, who was now coughing into her palms. "This room is designated for girls who... don't want to live anymore."

"What?" I asked.

"Girls who need protection for their families, or for their kids. Girls who owe big and can't pay it off. She's here to die." Rick spoke softly, as if we were in a museum.

"How do they—?"

"I'm done!" The woman crammed her hand into her mouth. In awe, I watched as she fisted her face hole. She pinched her eyes together and blew her nose. Streams of snot poured out.

"Oh my... God!" I proclaimed and watched helplessly. She worked her fist down her mouth and toward her throat. I could only imagine how much it hurt. Her throat began to swell beneath her chin, reminding me of a bullfrog.

"Watch!" Rick's hand clasped the back of my head and held it steady, forcing me to take in the sight of her bizarre suicide, whether I wanted to see them or not.

She cranked her head back and slammed her arm in—*deep*. The sounds she made weren't dissimilar from those an achy boat motor makes when it's struggling to start. More goblets of snot fell out of her ruddy nose. Her eyes had gone pink, and her hair lay flat against her sweaty scalp.

"What's she doing?" I asked, even though I already knew.

She pulled her arm out from her throat, dragging her insides up. A long sheath of red and pink tissue came out, clumped between her fingers and hanging out from her yawning mouth. She had grabbed a handful of her esophageal lining and had pulled it free.

I could see a map of blue veins woven through the pink inner-flesh.

She released a sound that was as wet and as gross as a boot plunging into a mud puddle. Then she reached up with her other hand and took a firm hold on the strands of musculature hanging out of her. With a hard yank, she seemed to have pulled a cork free. The organs came out of her as easily as a loose string from a sweater. With both hands, she upheaved her guts, holding and coddling them as they leaked out from her open mouth.

She collapsed onto the ground, unleashing a volley of blood onto the plastic tarp. It poured out like a stream. More blood than I had thought was possible.

I covered my mouth, tasting her bile and my semen between my pudgy fingers. Rick held me firm and kept my gaze affixed on the dying woman we had just fucked. The woman who had offered her services to us out of desperation. The woman who had ended her life here... all for our amusement. I didn't even know her name.

And all I can think, I'm sorry to admit, was one thing. Which I told Rick, much to his abysmal pleasure. I looked at him out of the corner of my eyes and I said:

"I want to do it again."

Rick smiled. A long and slender grin which reminded me of a crocodile. He removed his hand from the back of my head and placed it between my shoulder blades.

"You're the first person who's ever said that to me." He said, wistfully.

What could I say? We were both sick.

Absolutely... diseased.

Wee-Gee

"A *what*? A 'Ooh-Wa-Jah board'?"

"Nah. It's pronounced 'Wee-Gee'." Phillip Caster crossed his arms and beamed with pride. "I thought it'd be perfect for the party!"

"Huh. Some party. There's only gonna be you, me, Kirk, and Doug. Not exactly a 'rager'." Lincoln Arthur picked the box up and flipped it over so he could examine his backside. "Where'd you even get this thing?"

"It was my uncles. You know, during the funeral, I snuck around his house and—err—grabbed a couple things."

"You stole a Ouija board from a dead person. Seems smart." Lincoln laced his words with sarcasm.

"He had a lot of cool stuff. My mom always said: 'my brother was an odd duck'. I think what she meant was... Uncle Trey was a wizard!" Phillip exclaimed.

"Like Merlin?" Lincoln raised his brows.

Phillip shrugged. "Well... you'll see. I found a ton of crazy stiff."

TOXIC

Lincoln and Phillip had been buddies since grade school. The party—if it could even be called that—was Phil's idea. They were going to hold this last sleepover before summer was over and they were officially in high-school. At that point, they figured that the four of them would be too old for slumber parties and kid's games. They'd be too busy going to "real" parties, and—hopefully—meeting girls.

The shindig was going to be held at Lincoln's house. His folks were out of town, and he was the only member of their gang that didn't have annoying little siblings. His brother was in the Navy, so there was no chance for him intruding on their fun! Besides—and this was unspoken—Lincoln was the wealthiest of their herd. His three-story house was located in the woods, on a sprawling estate. Lincoln's bedroom was about the size of Phillip's apartment, and it featured a home-gym, a titanic flatscreen TV, and even a snack bar. It was no question that Lincoln's house was ideal for get-togethers and hangouts.

Lincoln was also the group's unofficial leader. He was only a few months older than Kirk, but he was a whole year older than Doug and Phillip. Doug was the youngest. He was a bespectacled nerd who'd skipped the fourth grade. Despite his acne, his nasally voice, and his offensive bowl-cut, Doug was a good kid and Phillip considered him a pal. And Phillip was best friends with Lincoln, even if Lincoln wasn't exactly best friends with Phillip. But Phillip didn't want anything to do with Kirk.

The boy was trouble.

TOXIC

Last year, he'd been suspended for bringing a dead groundhog into the gymnasium and putting a firecracker up its rear. The smoke had summoned the fire department. Phillip hadn't been around to see the aftereffects, but he had heard about it from Doug.

"He took the thing out of his backpack and just... lobbed it onto the basketball court. Like a Molotov cocktail! It blew up before anyone could even run. I saw black gunk splatter all over Mindy Keeling's legs! *Yeech!*"

"I dunno. I thought it was funny." Lincoln had said, defending his buddy. "But he's grounded for a month."

'He's lucky that's all he got." Doug squeaked. "You know, he coulda been in some serious trouble! Jail time!"

"Don't be dramatic. It was just a prank." Lincoln rolled his eyes.

But Phillip didn't think it was a very funny prank. Kirk's humor ran dark. Two years prior, the Columbine shooting had happened. It had rocked the country and made parents distrustful of outcasted youths. Kirk's response event was to use a permanent marker on a white tee shirt. His message read: "I Luv Dylan & Eric". He had come to school wearing a trench coat and cheap sunglasses along with his perverse tee.

Kirk had revealed to Lincoln—and Lincoln alone—that the back of his shirt had read: "Shoot Every Student". But he had kept that piece of the joke hidden beneath his offensive coat.

Kirk was taller than anyone else in the group, and louder. If they were doing something dangerous, Kirk was likely the conceiver of the idea.

He'd gotten Doug—the smallest and skinniest of the herd—to crawl through a drainpipe once, after convincing him that he'd seen someone drop a wallet down it.

He'd gotten Phillip to shoplift a nudie magazine before, only to yell: "thief!" right as the two approached the store's exit.

He'd even brought booze to their crumbling fort behind the school. It had once been a garden shed, but they'd converted it into a clubhouse. It was located deep in the woods, so no one from the school's staff knew about it. They kept empty bottles, illicit magazines, comics, and even a pack of moldy cigarettes in there. It was a shitty place to hang out in though, and they only used it when they were sure that they wouldn't be awarded any privacy at Lincoln's house. Without insulated walls, the clubhouse was always too hot or too cold.

No. Phillip thought, circling back on track. *Lincoln's place is much better than that stuffy ol' clubhouse.*

They were currently sitting in Lincoln's living room. Phillip was wearing a Marilyn Manson shirt—which his mother abhorred—and a pair of shorts. His blonde hair was rucked back with oil. He'd taken to smoothing it back like a crispy '50's greaser. It was a look his father told him he'd regret, which only made him commit to it more.

Lincoln was sitting on the edge of his bed, holding a baseball in his hands. Every now and again, he'd toss the ball from one hand to the other; like an unimpressive juggler. He was round, and his head was shorn almost bald.

Laying on the floor, ahead of Phillip's crossed legs, was the Ouija board and a black cloth sack stuffed with goodies.

Phillip opened the bag and dug into it. His fingers scrabbled over bizarre trinkets and items.

"You didn't just buy these at the trick shop, did ya?" Lincoln asked. "They really came from your uncle's house?"

"Cross my heart." Phillip confirmed. "Look at this!" He pulled out a small booklet. It was about the size of a pocket-bible, with a similar leathery cover. He opened it up and showed its contents to Lincoln.

"What's in it?" The wealthier boy crawled off his bed, leaving the baseball floating on the rumbled covers like a buoy.

Lincoln took the book and scanned the pages. "It's just symbols... and cursive. It isn't in English. What is this? Latin?"

"I dunno." Phillip shrugged. "Maybe Doug will!"

"Doug's a brainiac but I don't think he speaks dead languages." Lincoln snorted.

"Ya never know." Phillip took out the next item. It was a small crystal. Pink and bright.

"They sell those at the health store. You know? They say they can—like—fix your aura or somethin'." Lincoln chittered.

"Maybe. It's real pretty." Phillip held the crystal up and turned it in the light. It sparkled like sweat.

"What are you? A girl?" Lincoln chuffed.

Embarrassed, Phillip stowed the object back into the bag. "Well, not all of it is that interesting, but the board definitely is." Phillip insisted.

"We'll have to play with it for sure. Bet it'll freak Doug out." Lincoln sneered.

Phillip hoped that Lincoln wasn't going to follow Kirk's lead and start harassing Doug. The poor kid was picked on enough at school, he didn't need to be bullied by his "friends". Phillip also didn't want to be put in a situation where he was required to stand up for the littler kid. Phillip didn't want to upset Kirk and Lincoln. He felt that doing so would set a target on his own back.

Are these boys really your friends? A niggling voice pestered him. It rose up whenever Kirk and Lincoln were being especially cruel. Like when they'd climbed a tree to pluck bird eggs out of a nest, just to pop them in their fingers for laughs. Or the day they had gone down a street, opening mailboxes and scattering envelopes on the ground.

Are they really your friends, Phillip? The voice shifted and changed. It became his mother. Hearing the question from her made the answer easy.

Yes, they were Phillip's friends. Because his parents disapproved of them, that made them cool.

Phillip liked being around Lincoln—at least, he liked it when Kirk wasn't around. Lincoln was always quick to make a good joke, and he had a lot of cool things in his house. For Phillip's underdeveloped mind... that was enough to make Lincoln his best friend for life.

×

Doug arrived at the 'party' first. His mother deposited him in front of the door, then sped off. The woman always seemed to be happy to be rid of the little boy. Phillip helped Doug carry an armload of chips, sodas, and candies into the house.

"You know, you don't have to bring all this stuff every time you come over. Lincoln's got a full pantry." Phillip said as he held the door open for Doug.

"I know. But Grandma always told me 'If you're going to a party, be sure to bring cake'!" Doug was filled with anachronistic quotes from his deceased grandma. Phillip theorized that the older woman had been his only friend, until the gang picked him up.

They brought the snacks down to Lincoln's room. The older boy hadn't left his bed after Doug had rang the doorbell. He'd simply remained reclined, with a comic book open in his hands.

Doug walked over to the bed and laid the snacks out on the floor. Despite having a snack bar, a gym, and a bathroom the size of Phillip's bedroom, the children had decided it was best to be as near the bed as possible.

Lincoln gave Doug a curt nod. "Wassup, little dude?"

Doug adjusted his glasses. "Hey, is that the new *Spawn*?"

"Nah. It's last week's issue. You can have it when I'm done"

"Thanks. I've already read it though." Doug said. He was always up-to-date on the new comic books.

"When's Kirk coming over?" Phillip asked, cutting in.

"*Homo* said he'd be riding his bike. His dad's working doubles this week." Lincoln jeered.

Phillip wondered if Kirk would be better behaved if his parents were more present. Like Doug's mom, Kirk's folks seemed to want to keep their own boy at arm's length.

"What's that?" Doug pointed toward the items left behind on the floor.

"It's wizard shit." Lincoln said, before Phillip could respond. "Phil's uncle was into occult stuff. Look at this." He picked the Ouija board up and showed its face to Doug.

The smaller boy gulped.

"Whats the matter?" Lincoln cooed. "Are you scared?"

"N-no." Doug said. "I just don't know if we should be playing with a dead guys stuff is all."

"Ah, it'll be cool, man." Phillip said, patting Doug on the back. "We'll wait until it's dark and we can ask it some silly questions. We don't have to take it seriously."

"I guess."

Outside, rain began to patter. Legs of liquid stampeded down the windows in Lincoln's room.

TOXIC

"It's raining? Already? Gee. I hope Kirk makes it here fine." Doug asked.

"What snacks did you bring?" Lincoln hefted himself out of his bed, leaving the dog-eared comic on the bedsheets.

"Sno-Balls, Nutter Butters, Zebra—"

"Oh, fuck yeah. I love Zebra Cakes." Lincoln took the box from the pile and tore it open, digging around for a pack of sugary cakes. He scarfed the candy down with a lopsided grin.

"I really hope Kirk's okay." Doug said.

"He's fine. Unless he tracks mud through my house. Then... I'll kill him." Lincoln joked.

As if they had conjured him, the three boys heard the doorbell ring. This time, Lincoln went up with them.

Kirk was wet. His bike lay discarded in the paved driveway, and he was holding his arms around his chest. His red hair lay like stringy pasta over her brow. His green bomber jacket was torn at the shoulder. He claimed to have been hit with a bullet while out hunting with his dad and his older brother, but everyone knew that story was bullshit.

"Lemme in!" Kirk dived through them and stamped into the house. He was quick to remove his shoes and tear his jacket away from his shoulders. "God! I'm soaked! Jesus!"

"You look like you just got out of the pool." Doug chuckled.

"And you look like a soiled diaper. What's it to ya?" Kirk sneered. His tone was hard to gauge, so Phillip was relieved when Kirk socked Doug in the arm and said: "I'm just joshin' ya, squirt. Hey, we got any frozen pizza in this shit-hole? I've got the munchies."

"No, but mom left behind some cash." Lincoln said. "Wanna order in?"

"Let's!"

×

While they ate their four pizzas—one cheese, one pepperoni, one sausage and mushroom, and one carnivore special—they decided to watch a movie in the family room. Phillip thought that the term "cathedral" was more accurate. The massive room was almost overwhelming, and the entertainment center made Lincoln's TV look like a dwarf.

Phillip told Kirk about the Ouija board. The disheveled boy shrugged and said: "Cool. You get anything else off of him? Like, an inheritance?"

Phillip pursed his lips. "Mom and dad did, but I didn't know Uncle Trey all that well. I saw him at—like—family stuff. But no... he didn't leave me any money."

"Bummer. When my grandpa died some of his cash went into my college fund." Kirk sneered. "Wish I could have it myself though." Kirk turned his attention to Lincoln. "Hey, you ever get the nudie channels on this thing?"

The boys were sprawled out on all corners of the room, occupying whichever piece of furniture suited their fancy; but not so far away that they would feel isolated.

"Nah. I mean, my dad would definitely notice if I started tuning in on that shit. But this movie is pretty good." Lincoln said. "It's got boobies in it."

"Yeah. In *one* scene." Kirk rolled his eyes and pantomimed shooting himself in the head.

Doug snickered.

Phillip had been enjoying the movie, and he was glad everyone had decided that a horror flick would be appropriate. Especially considering their late-night plans.

The Ouija board was resting on his mind like overdue homework. He couldn't wait to try it out.

He had considered taking it on a test run at home. He'd chickened out after setting his hands on the planchette. Not that Phillip would ever admit such a wimpy maneuver to his pals.

On the screen, a maniacal slasher was shoving a decapitated head into a toilet.

"This is the best part." Lincoln said, shushing his pals.

They watched as the killer lowered his trousers, sat on the toilet, and began to fart loudly.

"Christ!" Kirk laughed.

"Why did we decide to eat while watching this?" Doug set his half-chewed slice of pizza back in its box.

"Weak." Kirk chuckled. "You do know it's all fake, right?"

"Yeah. It's just gross." Doug said.

Kirk peeled a layer of cheese off his pizza, then licked up the tomato paste. He grinned toward Doug, letting the red sauce leak between his teeth.

TOXIC

"Har-har." Doug crossed his arms.

"You want some chocolate ice cream?" Kirk wiped his lips with his wrist. "I'm sure Lincoln's got some. Extra chunky, with fudge sauce?"

"Nice try."

"You guys are gonna miss the good part." Lincoln pointed at the screen.

After the movie, Lincoln and Phillip played a few lazy rounds of ping-pong in Mr. Arthur's study. The room reminded Lincoln of the billiards rooms he saw in old movies, only instead of a pool table, they had ping-pong.

Kirk sat at Mr. Arthur's desk. He knew he wasn't allowed to touch Lincoln's dad's papers or his computer monitor. For once, Kirk followed the rules. He twirled around on the office chair but was careful not to molest anything that could get Lincoln in trouble.

Doug sat on the ground, hypnotized by the ball as it *thunk*-ed from paddle to paddle.

"I'm bored." Kirk said.

Phillip sighed. He was finally starting to get into the game.

"What are we doing? Waiting until midnight? Let's go check out the dead dude's Ouija board." Kirk insisted. Behind him, the window was streaked with rainwater. It was really pouring now. Every now and again, a flicker of lightning would startle the boys, and a low rumble of thunder would chill them.

"Yeah. Let's go play with it." Lincoln caught the ping-pong ball midair.

TOXIC

Phillip nodded. "Okay. You sure?" he couldn't believe he'd asked it. He expected to be hounded for being a "wimp".

Instead, Kirk stood and cracked his knuckles. "It's perfect now, ain't it? Hey! What if the power goes out? I think Douggie would crap his panties!"

"Would not!" The younger boy said.

"Would to!" Kirk chortled.

"Okay, okay." Lincoln said. "Let's do this, huh? C'mon, guys."

×

In Lincoln's room, they all got to work "setting the mood". Lincoln raced up to the pantry and came back with two wax candles, which he quickly lit.

"Won't those leave a mess without holders?" Doug asked.

Lincoln shrugged. "I'll just get Bernice to clean it up." He was referring to the long-suffering housemaid that took the bus to their property every other day.

The candles were thick and stocky. They burned brightly.

Doug flicked the lights off, and the massive room was cast in an amber glow. It made Phillip feel as if he was in a cave rather than a wealthy estate. He let a shiver creep up his spine and settle between his shoulders.

"Check this out, Doug! Phil and I were wondering if you could read this." Lincoln pulled the leatherbound book from the black sack and tossed it toward Doug. Doug fumbled with the book, and Phillip worried he'd drop it directly onto one of the two candles, igniting it.

After managing to keep ahold of it, Doug sat down on the floor with a grunt. He held the opened book beside the candle and scanned its pages. "I don't know. Some of this looks... Euclidian."

"Is that like... Latin?" Lincoln asked.

"No. It's more like... math." Doug shrugged. "Geometry."

"Oh. Snore." Kirk muttered.

"Yeah. This is *definitely* math. I dunno. It's from Uncle Trey?" Doug asked.

"Everything from this bag is. I found it with the Ouija board in his closet. I—we were eating dinner after the funeral at Aunt Martha's. Before she moved. There was all sorts of stuff lying around from Uncle Trey. I doubt I'm the only person that took something. The house was crowded."

"No one noticed you walking out with all this stuff?" Doug pressed.

"Nope. I didn't even notice I had taken it until we were back home, and I was walking into my bedroom with it. I dunno, man. The whole vibe around the funeral was weird. I kind of hoped I'd learn more about who Uncle Trey was but... no one really wanted to talk about him. They were all more concerned about Aunt Martha. Even during the sermon, no one talked about Trey directly. They just spoke about all the people he knew and his family. It was weird. And his son was there. My cousin, I guess. I don't know him all that well. Odd guy. People seemed to avoid him."

"What made him so odd?" Kirk asked, interested now.

"I dunno." Phillip scratched the back of his head. "He was wearing a suit but... he looked dirty. Scuffed. Homeless. Like he'd been sleeping outside. And he didn't seem to want to talk to anybody. He just sat in the corner and ate like he'd never eaten before when we were back at Martha's. He didn't even speak about his dad. He was... weird." Phillip trailed off.

The boys sat in mystified silence.

"You're pulling our legs." Kirk eventually wagered.

"Cross my heart. It's all true." Phillip insisted. "My cousin, Carl, is a weird guy, and so was Uncle Trey."

"What was he like? Trey?" Doug looked up from the book of geometric shapes and symbolic language. His eyes were already strained from being made to read by candlelight.

"I don't know. I never got to know him. Mom kept us pretty far from Trey and Martha. She always said they were 'strange', but that was it. Maybe she knew about all this weird shit he kept around." Phillip pointed toward the black bag. "Look at the rest of the stuff in there."

Lincoln turned the bag over and scattered the objects out in the middle of their circle. There was a planchette for the board. It was spade shaped, and it had a circular hole in its center. There was the pink crystal, a loop of leather, and a handful of other items.

"Wow. What's this?" Kirk reached down and picked up a slender crucifix. On it lay a figure of Christ, only its head was shaped like a goat with two corkscrew horns.

"I dunno. Looks like some Satan shit." Lincoln said, taking the crucifix and turning it upside down. "Oh! Look at this!"

Lincoln took the leather loop and pushed it through a hole notched into the bottom of the cross. He held it out so all could observe.

It was a pendant.

Struck with inspiration, Phillip picked up the pink crystal and held it up beneath the swaying pendant. He took ahold of it and fit the crystal between the tips of the horns. They wedged into the rock's grooves and held it tightly.

"Whoa! It's like... the devil's Legos!" Kirk honked.

"They all go together." Phillip swallowed.

He removed his hands and watched as the pendant swung like a pendulum from Lincoln's fist.

"That's wild." Lincoln said, taking the crucifix and holding it by the candle. The crystal glowed brightly between the goat-horns.

"Look! It's in the book!" Doug pointed toward the last page of the manuscript. On it, an ink drawing of the pendant was shown, just as the boys had manufactured.

"It's the only part that's in English too. *Ahem.*" Doug pulled the book back and read in a stilted voice: "'*A Divining Jewel can help find what is lost. All one needs is a Blood Stone, and a figurehead of Lord Satan, as well as a mobile strap.'* That's crazy. You guys know what a 'Divining Rod' is, right?"

"The only rod I know about is what's in my pants." Kirk tried to joke, but nobody took the bait.

"No. What is it?" Lincoln asked.

"It's what people used to use in the old days to find water. They'd take a Y-shaped stick, and let it guide them. It was like... psychic stuff."

"So, this thing is like that?" Lincoln held Uncle Trey's pendant up for emphasis. "If we follow it it'll lead us to—like—an underground spring?"

'I doubt it." Doug said. "I mean, if it really works... I don't think it's supposed to find water. It seems a bit more complicated than that."

"Maybe it led Satanists to virgins and shit. Don't they sacrifice virgins?" Kirk asked. "If so, Douggie's in danger!"

"I'm not a virgin!" Doug snapped. "I kissed Wendy Anne!"

"Yuh. In kindergarten! And kissin' don't count. You know that!"

"Shut up, guys." Phillip said. "Get serious. Are we saying that... Uncle Trey was a satanist?"

"I don't see any other alternative. You said it yourself." Lincoln said. "He could be a wizard!"

"Yeah. A wizard. Not a... *satanist!*" Phillip stated.

"What's the difference?" Lincoln asked.

"I dunno! I just can't imagine Uncle Trey... worshiping the devil and sacrificing babies and shit!"

"You said you didn't know him all that well." Doug said.

Phillip knew they were right. All the evidence was pointing toward something unsavory. Still, there was a difference between having fun with a Ouija board and worshiping the devil.

At school, a speaker had come over to talk about the dangers of rock music. He linked it to the Columbine shooting and to the general degeneracy of Phillip's generation. During the man's impassioned speech, Phillip had wondered if it was illegal for someone to preach about God and the Devil in a school setting. Now, he was retroactively mad that the speaker had blamed the youths, while old guys like Uncle Trey were *actually* worshiping Satan.

"We should ask the Ouija board about it." Kirk cut in.

"Huh?" Doug asked.

"Ask the Ouija board if we could talk to Uncle Trey. Maybe, he'll be able to explain what he was into!"

"Yeah! That's not a bad idea!" Lincoln tossed the crucifix across the circle. Phillip nabbed it from the air and instinctually opened the leather loop. Before he could stop himself, he tossed it over his head and let the crucifix dangle ahead of his breast.

Why'd you do that? Phillip asked himself. *And why aren't you taking it off?*

Lincoln set the board at the center of their circle, then took the planchette in his hands. He laid the spade-shaped tool on the board, then set his index fingers upon it. "Like this, right?"

"I guess so. Did Trey leave instructions behind?" Doug asked.

"No." Phillip answered. "No. Just the board."

"I saw some kids play with one of these in a movie before." Kirk said. "I think you're not allowed to take your hands off the thingamajig unless someone says 'goodbye'."

"Cool. But how do we start?" Lincoln asked.

"Let's all just... touch the thing." Phillip reached out and imitated Lincoln, setting his index fingers on the planchette. Kirk and Doug followed suit.

"Okay. Now what?" Doug asked.

"Let's just... ask if anyone is there." Phillip coughed. The pendant felt heavy around his neck. The pink crystal tilted toward the Ouija board, as if it was drawn to it. "H-hello? Is anyone out there?"

The boys held their breath.

"Nothing is happening." Kirk said, startling his pals.

"Maybe we need a magic word." Lincoln offered.

"I could check the book." Doug said. "Maybe there's some more English hidden in with all the crazy symbols—"

"No." Phillip stated firmly. "Don't take your fingers off the planchette."

"The... what?" Kirk asked.

"The *thing*."

"If nothing is happening, then I don't think it should matter." Kirk laughed.

"It might. I don't think we should risk it. Not until we're sure." Phillip continued.

"Okay. Fine. Whatever." Kirk rolled his eyes.

"Phil is right." Lincoln scolded. "We should take this seriously."

"I thought this was supposed to be fun." Kirk said.

"I don't know." Lincoln said. "With the lights off and the Satan shit... I don't know."

Doug coughed, drawing everyone's attention toward him. "I think I know what to say."

"Okay. God for it." Lincoln said.

Doug sucked in a breath, closed his eyes, and said: "Hello. Is Uncle Trey here?"

The planchette zipped across the board, pulling their hands with it. The circle in the spade's center landed over the word "YES" on the board's corner.

"Whoa!" Kirk barked. "Who did that?"

"Not me!" Doug gasped.

"It was one of you! This is dumb! Yer all just tryna' scare me! It ain't workin'!"

"Don't take your hands off the board!" Lincoln warned.

"Fuck off!" Kirk continued.

"Shut up! Shut up, guys!" Phillips said. "Let's just ask it... him another question."

'What? You really think you're talking to your dead uncle? Get off it, Phil!" Kirk continued.

"Uncle Trey... were you a Satanist?"

The planchet tore across the board and circled back to "YES".

"Oh my God." Phillip muttered.

TOXIC

"C'mon. If one of you is doing this, just lemme know. I won't even be mad." Kirk stated.

"I'm not!" Doug insisted.

"Let's test it to make sure it's really him. How'd you die, Uncle Trey? Phillip hasn't told us."

The truth was, Phillip didn't know. His uncle's passing was as much a mystery to him as it was to his pals.

The planchette zipped across the board, and Doug read out the letters it hovered over. "M-U-R-D-E-R-E-D."

Their faces went pale.

"Is that true, Phillip?" Lincoln asked.

"I don't know." Phillip susurrated. "I don't know."

"W-who murdered you, Sir?" Lincoln asked.

Doug once again acted as translator. "C-A-R-L."

"My cousin?" Phillip's jaw dropped.

"The weird, dirty, homeless dude?" Kirk asked.

"Why would he kill you, Uncle Trey?" Phillip was now immersed. He fully believed that they were using the Ouija board to communicate to a ghost. Even if one of his pals told him they'd been pushing the planchette, Phillip doubted he'd believe them. "Why'd he kill you?"

Doug read: "T-O O-P-E-N T-H-E D-O-O-R."

"What door?" Lincoln asked.

"This is stupid." Kirk interjected. "That doesn't even make sense. Why would you need to kill someone just to open a fuckin' door?"

Doug read: "T-H-E B-E-Y-O-N-D."

"See? It's just nonsense now. That doesn't mean anything!" Kirk continued.

TOXIC

"Does it have to do with the Divining Jewel?" Phillip asked.

"T-H-E K-E-Y."

"The key? The Divining Jewel is a key? A key to the door?"

"T-H-E B-E-Y-O-N-D."

The planchette was racing across the board now, respelling its message for emphasis.

"I don't understand, Uncle Trey. Please, explain it to us. Where is the door? Is it back at your house?" Phillip asked.

"T-H-E D-O-O-R C-A-N B-E A-N-Y-W-H-E-R-E."

"I'm done with this." Kirk yanked his hands away from the planchette.

"No!" Doug and Lincoln shouted in unison.

Phillip almost screamed when two pale hands broke out from the shadows and wrapped around Kirk's chest, holding his arms at his side. The hands were snow-white, and each digit ended in a painted, red nail.

Kirk butted his head back, and another hand grabbed him by the hair, tugging at his scalp and pulling the creases smooth on his brow.

Kirk screamed like a little girl. The rest of the boys held their hands on the planchette, terrified that the hands would grasp them if they moved their fingers away from it.

"Stop it! Stop it! Doug, I'm sorry I rag on you all the time! Please! Make them stop! This isn't funny! Please!" Kirk screeched, obviously believing this to be a cruel prank orchestrated by his pals. Tears broke away from his eyes and glittered on his cheeks. In the flickering candlelight, his movements were jarring. It was as if he had been turned into a stop-motion puppet.

Another two hands *whooshed* out from the shadows. They hooked their fingers into the sides of Kirk's mouth and pulled his lips into a grotesquely forced smile. Kirk began to hyperventilate, choking on his own screams.

"Please! Let him go, Uncle Trey!" Phillip pleaded with the board. "He's sorry he didn't believe! Just let him go!"

The planchette moved.

"N-O-T M-E."

"Oh, Jesus!" Kirk screamed as another two hands slid out of the shadows. These ones held daggers with ornate hilts and curved blades. The smooth weapons glimmered in the candlelight, dripping with moisture and stained with blood.

"Oh, God!" Kirk screamed.

Mechanically, the bladed hands fell back and drove their tools into his eyeballs. There was an instantaneous gush of blood. Phillip could *hear* the bulbs pop in his pal's skull. The blades were driven in to their hilts, crunching through Kirk's eyes and scratching his brain. The boy's screams were replaced with mewling moans.

"N-O-T M-E." Uncle Trey wrote. "T-H-E D-E-M-O-N-S!"

Kirk was dragged back into the shadows. He was swallowed by darkness, giving only one last panicked shriek before he was totally gone. All that remained of Kirk were the droplets of blood he had squirted across the Ouija board.

In stunned silence, the boys remained in place around the board.

"D-did that really just happen?" Lincoln asked.

The planchette zoomed over to "YES".

"Oh." Doug muttered. "Is he... dead?"

The planchette rushed over to "NO". A few seconds ticked by, then it moved over to "YES".

"We need to stop this. We need to stop this. I don't want to play anymore. I wanna go home. I wanna call my Momma and go home." Doug whispered.

"I don't think we can stop. What if we say 'goodbye' and it doesn't work? Then... those *things* will get us." Phillip theorized.

"Fuck. Why'd you bring this thing over here?" Lincoln rasped.

"I didn't know it would do... *that!*" Phillip said.

The planchette zipped across the board.

"N-O-T Y-O-U-R F-A-U-L-T P-H-I-L."

"Oh, yeah? Who's fault is it?" Lincoln asked.

"C-A-R-L."

"Why? Why is this his fault? Because he murdered you?" Phillip asked.

"H-E W-A-N-T-S T-O O-P-E-N T-H-E D-O-O-R B-U-T H-E C-A-N-T Y-O-U H-A-V-E T-H-E K-E-Y."

The pendant felt even heavier around Phillip's neck. He swallowed deeply, wishing he could take his hands off the planchette so he could tear the pendant away from his throat and cast it into the shadows.

Maybe it would end up wherever Kirk's corpse was.

Phillip still couldn't believe that his friend was dead, but he had witnessed it himself. The knives being plunged into Kirk's eye-sockets played on repeat in Phillip's head, like a film stuck in a loop.

This shouldn't be happening. We're just kids. We just wanted to play a game and have some fun tonight. We shouldn't be... dying. Phillip thought in a panic. *It's not fair!*

Doug asked the next question, and it was one Phillip wished he'd thought of. "H-how do we use the key?"

Uncle Trey's gravelly voice boomed across the dark room, causing the boys to shudder.

"The Beyond demands... BLOOD."

"Who is that? Holy shit! What the fuck!" Lincoln moaned.

"That's Trey!" Phillip explained. "Oh, God! That's his voice!"

The candles seemed to explode upward, filling the room with a sudden burst of ghastly illumination. Phillip saw that they had been transported. They no longer sat in the center of Lincoln's room. Instead, they were in the middle of a cavern. The walls were greased and glittery, and the ceiling was fashioned from eroded stone. Stalactites and stalagmites jutted up from all corners of the cathedral.

There were bodies as well.

Pulverized by stone mallets, a few corpses lay nearby. One was turned onto its back and its head was tilted toward Phillip's direction. He could see that its features had been mashed into its skull. Pulpy strands of garbled flesh hung from the decimated bones. Gooey blood coagulated in a halo beneath the molested head.

"The Beyond... demands... BLOOD!" Uncle Trey cried once again.

Following the voice, Phillip observed his uncle's fate. The man was welded to a wall. The stone seemed to grow around him, securing him in place.

A demon stood before him. The creature was tall, white-fleshed, and each finger ended in a red hook. The demon's face was compacted with cobwebs, which pulled in and out with the mummified monster's breaths. Its eyes were hollow sockets. It moved like a zombie, shambling on bleeding feet. It carried a long wooden javelin ahead of it. The javelin ended with a curved prong.

The demon drove the lance into Uncle Trey's guts.

The older man whined as blood spurted out from the wound and crawled down the shaft of the weapon. He sealed his eyes shut and bared his teeth. Blood seeped between his chompers and dribbled down his chin.

The demon twirled the lance, digging in with the pronged tip of the tool. He then jerked the javelin back, dredging out a payload of twisted innards. The organs slithered out of Uncle Trey's belly and splattered against the floor. They wheezed, hissed, and farted loudly against the cave's surface. Wriggling like snakes, the organs seemed to be attempting to run away now that they had been freed from Trey's chambers.

The demon turned its cobwebbed face toward the boys.

It cocked its head curiously.

Then, it reached up and drew the cobwebs aside like a bridal veil.

Kirk's eyeless face peered out from behind the demon's mask.

"It hurts." Kirk said. "It hurts... forever."

He drove the lance in once more, burying it deep in Trey's gut.

Uncle Trey began to cough loudly. Blood tore from his throat and spattered across Kirk's distorted face—

—the candles dimmed, and Phillip was thrust back into Lincoln's room—

—just as a machete *thwack*-ed into Doug's head.

"Holy shit!" Lincoln leapt away from the board, taking his fingers away from the planchette. Phillip's eyes danced from Doug's split head to Lincoln's fumbling body. It was too much to take in all at once.

Doug tilted forward. Blood splashed onto the board, warming Phillip's fingers. Phillip pressed down hard on the planchette, determined not to release his hold on it.

"Phillip! Help!" Lincoln called.

Phillip turned his head, trembling as he took in what had happened to Lincoln. The older boy was lying on the ground. Serrated fingers clutched him by the hair, pulling his head back and exposing his face to the candlelight.

"Phil." Lincoln grated. "I don't want to die—"

A pale hand shot out and slammed into the back of Lincoln's head. It punched into the skull and burst through the child's face, splitting it open. A rush of scrambled brain matter and bone chips spattered the floor and stippled the board.

The hand opened like a grotesque flower, then zipped backward, pulling its hooked nails through the remains of Lincoln's face. When the white hand—now tattooed red with blood—receded into the shadows, it left a gaping cave in the center of Lincoln's skull.

More hands clutched Lincoln's corpse and dragged him into the darkness, leaving a crimson streak behind.

Once Lincoln was gone, Phillip realized how alone he was.

Phillip turned back toward Doug's corpse. It lay on the ground. The head had been cleaved in two neat halves. Blood pumped freely from the gorge, which ran through Doug's upper jaw.

Why did he die? Phillip thought with a start. *Why did the demons kill Doug? He didn't take his hands off the planchette!*

The planchette responded, as if he'd asked his question aloud.

"C-A-R-L K-I-L-L-E-D H-I-M."

But how? Phillip felt tears streak his cheeks. He bit his lower lip and stammered through his words: "B-b-but Carl isn't-t he-here."

"Yes, I am." Carl responded. His voice boomed like an explosion of thunder through the darkness. It ripped Phillip's psyche in half. The boy felt warm fluid race down his legs. "I've been hiding in your shadow ever since I saw you leave the funeral with my belongings, boy."

Phillip gasped hard. He felt as if a cigarette had been put out on his lungs. Fire raced through his throat and landed at the base of his tongue. It simmered there, drawing more tears from his overworked eyes. He wanted to believe that he was hallucinating, but he knew that Carl's proclamation had been as real as the blood that soused his hands and face.

Phillip wheeled around, glancing through the shadows in search of his adult cousin.

The man stepped into the candlelight. He was dressed exactly as he had been at Uncle Trey's funeral. His shabby suit was coated in dirt, and his beard was tangled. He looked like a bridge troll to young Phillip.

Stooping over, Carl clutched the handle of the machete and drew it away from Doug's head. When the blade came free, another shipment of blood squirted loose from the child's skull.

Carl wiped the machete on his sleeve, leaving gummy streaks of blood on his clothes. He smiled toward Phillip, exposing jagged, yellowed teeth.

"You took somethin' that was supposed ta be mine, boy. Shouldn't have done that."

"No. No. I'm sorry. I just thought it'd be fun to play with! I'm sorry!" Phillip moaned.

"Not the board, you moron." Carl knelt down in front of Phillip and tapped the swinging pendant with the tip of his machete. "My key. The Blood Stone. It was promised to me, but Daddy hid it before I killed him. But I knew it'd wind up in your hands eventually. So, I watched you at the funeral. I watched as you followed his Magick commands... and took the pendant out of the house with you."

"Wh-what?" Phillip asked, confused by the events splayed out ahead of him.

"Oh, yes. He told me, as I drove the knife into his heart... that *you'd* make a better wizard than *me*. But it looks like he was wrong! You just treat these things like toys! Stupid boy! Ignorant child! You didn't even realize you were casting spells until Hell itself had displayed its glory to you!" Cousin Carl leaned in close. His breath smelled like iron, and his eyes were lined with pus. "My Daddy... was *wrong* about you!"

Phillip shook his head. "I-I didn't even know uncle—your dad. I didn't even know him!"

"Of course, you didn't. Your folks kept you away from Daddy after they caught him 'teaching' you spells when you were an infant. He always held out hope that you'd reconnect eventually. That is... before I came back and stabbed him in the fucking heart!" Carl sneered. "I don't know what he saw in you, boy. But *I'm* his son... so the Blood Stone is mine! It's my inheritance!"

Phillip looked down toward the board, hoping that his uncle would help him in his time of need. The planchette whisked across the board, landing over the word "NO".

"Wh-why did my friends have to die?" Phillip wheezed.

"Because demons demand blood. The Beyond... demands blood." Carl said. "Every single spell you cast requires it. Blood makes Magick run the way gas does a car. You'd know this, stupid boy, if you had spent any time with Daddy."

Carl pressed the wettened blade against the end of Phillip's chin. He felt his skin break. A trickle of blood raced down the blade's length.

"You need to give me the pendant, boy. Give me the Blood Stone."

Phillip shut his eyes. He began to pray that something would stop this man from menacing him. Anything.

"Give me... the Stone!" The man roared, spraying rancid spittle across Phillip's face. "Or I'll cut you in half the way I did your friend!"

In Phillip's mind, he saw the machete land once again on Doug's face, splitting it symmetrically. He then replayed Lincoln and Kirk's death. Knives through the eyes... a hand pushed through a head like a hot blade through butter—

I'm going to die. Phillip thought. *And I'll end up in Hell, where I'll be covered in spiderwebs and made to torture other souls. What did Kirk say? "It hurts... forever."* God. *I don't want to hurt! I don't want to go to Hell! I'm sorry! Please! I'm so sorry I don't listen to my parents, and I get into trouble with my friends, and I play with Ouija boards! Please, God! You can't let us die! We're just kids! We're just kids!*

God didn't answer Phillip's prayers. His uncle did.

While Carl pushed the blade into Phillip's chin, the boy felt his hands scrabble across the board, following the planchette. He peered down his upturned face and caught the words that his uncle was spelling.

"T-H-E B-E-Y-O-N-D N-E-E-D-S B-L-O-O-D!"

Phillip understood. He didn't know *how* it was that he came to understand exactly what Uncle Trey was telling him... but he *did*.

It came to him like a hammer hitting a nail into a wall.

The Beyond needs blood...

So, I have to give it blood...

And if I do... it will be withholden to me...

If Carl wants the key, he can't take it...

Because its mine...

The Blood Stone... is MINE!

Phillip took his fingers off the planchette. He squeezed his eyes closed, expecting the demonic hands to grope after him instantaneously, the way they had Lincoln and Kirk. Instead, he remained in his spot, sitting on his rump and tilting his head back as Carl pressed the machete into his chin.

"You're going to die, you ignorant *boy!*"

TOXIC

Three figures appeared behind Carl. Kirk, Lincoln, and Doug. They all retained the injuries they had borne in life. Kirk's eyes were hollow holes, Doug's face was split down the middle, and Lincoln's face was a black hole. The three boys wore long shrouds stitched from cobwebs and dust. They all carried lances, which ended in hooked prongs.

In unison, all three boys reared away, then plunged their weapons into Carl's back. They broke through, spraying blood into the air ahead of and behind the adult.

The machete slipped from Carl's hand and clattered against the stone floor of the Hell-Cave.

Carl's jaw dropped and his eyes rolled back into their socket. He released an orgasmic moan. Threads of blood fell from his mouth and corkscrewed through his bushy beard. "Oh... Oh, God!" Carl complained.

In one synchronized motion, the ghouls that had once been Phillip's friends pulled their lances loose. Gouts of blood spumed from the ragged holes in Carl's back. They stained the white cobwebs a heavy crimson.

The ghoulish boys dropped their weapons and fell upon Carl.

Phillip stood on creaky legs and stepped back, watching in awe as the children dug their hands into the wound.

"No... no!" Carl shouted, squirming in place. "Call them off, Phillip! Please! Tell them to stop! Tell them to stop!"

Doug pulled the flesh apart, allowing Kirk and Lincoln to reach into a widened hole in Carl's back.

"Oh, God! God! No!" Carl screeched, clawing at the ground. His unmanicured nails bent backward, breaking away from their bloody beds. "No!"

Lincoln hefted up the yellowed spinal cord. The segmented length of bones *thwipped* about like a fish pulled from water. Lincoln struggled to keep ahold of it, but he was helped by Kirk. With their hands secured around the spinal cord, both boys *tugged* hard.

Carl's head sank into his shoulders. His throat rumbled and his opened mouth cracked loudly. Phillip watched as the man's eyes turned white. Twin streams of blood broke from his nostrils and showered the ground.

Carl began to gargle animalistically. He scratched at the floor and kicked with his legs, as if he was attempting to swim away from a shark.

"Please! Phillip!" His voice was distorted by the violence that had been brought onto his body. Carl's throat was filled with liquid. His pus-rimmed eyes bulged from their sockets, threatening to pop loose. "I don't... wanna... die!" Carl moaned.

Phillip turned and ran screaming up the stairs and away from Lincoln's room. Behind him, he heard Carl gurgle as the ghouls dragged his mutilated body into the caves...

...into... the Beyond.

x

TOXIC

No one could tell what exactly had taken place in the Arthur house.

When Doug's mother came by to pick her son up the next day, she'd found Phillip Caster sitting on the porch. Half dead from the cold, he had sat unmoving in the rain for hours until morning.

Aware that something bad had happened, and alarmed by the blood streaked across Phillip's face, she'd barged into the house in search of her Douggie. She hadn't found the child, but she'd fainted upon spotting the splashes of blood in Lincoln's room. There was even gore hanging from the ceiling, like a fungal growth.

When the police were called, they were stumped. It was evident that something violent had occurred in the Arthur household, but Phillip Caster—the only survivor—was almost comatose. He simply shook his head when asked what had happened.

And all the while, he clutched a strange pendant which hung from his neck. He muttered to it, but his tone was garbled and indecipherable.

He refused to be separated from his pendant, so it was left around his neck.

When his parents finally arrived at the hospital, they rushed into his room and swaddled him with hugs and kisses. He'd been wiped clean with a sponge, but his flesh still tasted like child-blood.

"What happened?' His mother asked. "The cops said... said that there was a murder? But they couldn't—"

"I wouldn't advice asking him serious questions right now, Mrs. Caster. He's in an intense state of shock." A male doctor intruded. He was hovering around the bed, checking his clipboard incessantly. As if its contents would change between glances.

"We just want to know what happened!" Phillip's father insisted. "That's our son!"

"Yes. I know." The doctor continued. "But we must be gentle with him. When he's ready to speak, he will."

Phillip's eyes jittered from one face to another. He remembered what Carl had said about his mother forbidding his uncle from teaching Phillip the magical and satanic arts. Maybe, if she'd allowed him to continue his lessons, Phillip would've been more prepared for the horror-show he'd witnessed last night. Maybe, none of it would have even happened.

It's their fault. A growling voice proclaimed in Phillip's head. *Their fault... not yours. It's their fault that all your friends are—*

Phillip recalled how Lincoln, Kirk, and Doug had all died.

But he was also treated to new visions.

He saw the kids in the caverns of Hell, dragging Carl's crumpled body across the rocky ground, not caring that they were scraping the flesh from his bones. And despite the forceful removal of his spine and the deformation of his head, Carl was somehow still alive. He was pleading through broken lips:

"Please... I'm sorry... I'm sorry, Phillip... tell them to lemme go... please.."

TOXIC

He saw all of this, even while Phillip looked around his dismal hospital room. One image overlapped over the other. Hell was constant and omnipotent, no matter what the Bible had to say about it.

Slowly, Phillip said his first legible words since he'd been discovered on the front porch.

He looked up toward his teary-faced mother. He held the Blood Stone up against his lips. It was so hot; he could feel his saliva evaporating as he spoke:

"I am the key... to the door."

"What was that? Phillip? Huh? What did you say?" The woman asked, kneeling by his hospital bed.

Phillip's grip on the pendant was so tight, he could feel the edges of the crucifix digging into his skin. The Blood Stone *thrummed* with electric heat, like a stove top.

Phillip understood now that he had been called to pick the articles out of Uncle Trey's house during the funeral. It was his inheritance, not Carl's. Uncle Trey had left them all behind for Phillip to play with. He also understood that being gifted the Blood Stone meant that Phillip now held dominion over at least three of the residents of Hell.

It's their fault. Your parents kept you away from the Blood Stone. Away from me. You'd be a master of the Dark Arts by now if it wasn't for them. You should show them. You should show them what Hell is like! The voice in his head sounded like it belonged to Phillip himself, but it must have been coming from a doppelganger because the boy had never once thought such vile things about his parents before.

And yet...

He was mad at his parents. They belittled him, told him what to wear, and even critiqued his friends. Now, his pals were dead, and Phillip wondered if his mom and dad would celebrate when his back was turned—

I miss them. I want them back. Phillip thought. *I want my friends back. They didn't need to die. They didn't have to! It's not fair!*

He wondered, half curious and half terrified, if he could summon Lincoln, Kirk, and Doug at will. He had called them up to take care of Carl, after all. And they'd done the job with no complaints.

If Phillip controlled the Blood Stone, then that also meant... he controlled the Beyond.

No wonder Carl wanted this thing. The options are limitless.

Deluded with trauma, Phillip decided it would be fun to try the Blood Stone out, just to see if it really worked. He could summon up his pals, and they could play whatever games Phillip wanted. They wouldn't protest or bicker, he reasoned, because they'd just be happy to spread their hurt rather than hold it in.

"Phillip, hun? Can you tell me what you're thinking?" His mother cooed, intruding on his thoughts.

Phillip held the Blood Stone up to his mouth and said:

TOXIC

"Open the door."
All around him... the lights flickered...

Sally

He thought that this oughta be on record as the hottest day on earth. Pat just could not imagine it ever getting hotter or it ever having been as hot as it was on this afternoon.

He mopped his brow with his sleeve and let his tongue lull out of his mouth, like a dog's. Pat looked up through a lance of solid sunlight. His eyes blurred up, welling with tears.

Pat wiped his face. He wondered if he should take off his tweed jacket. It felt swampy with sweat. He dismissed the idea quickly. He had to keep the jacket. His momma had told him it made him look "smart", and if he was going to impress Sally, then Pat needed to look "smart".

"S-Sally, I h-hope you... cripes." He muttered.

He had been practicing in front of the mirror since he'd set his mind on asking Sally to marry him. The problem was, he'd yet to get through his pre-planned speech without stuttering.

"S-Sally... I's... uh... I hope yer doin' good today." Pat sighed. "Y-you sound like a b-bumpkin."

That was something his momma had called him before. She had a rolodex of insults *and* compliments, which she pulled from depending on the situation.

Pat shook his head and walked on, pushing through the humid atmosphere and the beams of sunlight. He felt as if he was swimming through hot tar. Pat wished he'd waited for a colder day to do all of this, but circumstances hadn't been helpful. No matter what, he had to ask Sally to marry him today.

He had to.

If he didn't ask her today, he'd never get another chance to. His momma was probably calling the cops right this second—

Nope.

He couldn't think like that.

Pat sighed heavily and continued his trek. He was walking to Sally's house, which was something of a hike. There was a gravel path that crawled through the forest like a centipede. It went alongside a scummy pond, then led up the hill where Sally lived.

Pat was striding beside the pond. Mosquitos flitted through the air around Pat. Clouds of gnats skittered over his opened mouth, clinging to the scraps of chapped skin hanging from his pink lips. Pat shook his head and waved a hand ahead of him.

He felt something pinch his palm. When he pulled his hand back, he caught a fattened bulb growing from it. He closed his hand into a fist, then opened it. The mosquito had turned into an oily smear.

TOXIC

Pat wiped the mosquito's body against the breast of his heavy jacket. "L-little... turd!" He muttered.

Instantly, Pat felt ashamed. He'd been raised not to hate, because every creature on earth was designed by God with a purpose. Although Pat didn't understand why God would make something as pesky as a mosquito. Or a gnat. Still, Pat felt like he should atone for his thoughts.

Pat stopped his trek. Sally was important, but God had to be appeased at all costs. If Pat didn't ask for forgiveness, God might influence Sally to say "no" when Pat popped the question.

He couldn't risk it.

Wringing his hands together, Pat dipped his head and prayed.

"Dear God, I's sorry fer making fun of that dang mo-skeeter. I know you love it as much as you love me, and I'm real sorry I done smooshed it and called it names. Please, Lord, forgive me. And please forgive me fer what I had to do to momma. Amen!"

Satisfied that he'd been forgiven, Pat lifted his head and smiled. To prove to God that he had meant every word of his prayer, he didn't even swat at the mosquito clinging to his cheek. The bug sucked away at him, causing his irritated skin to grow red and bumpy.

Jeez. I hope I don't scare Sally off! Pat thought as he continued his stroll. He let his noodle-y arms swing by his sides. He kicked at the gravel as he walked, whistling to himself. His exaggerated

TOXIC

movements took his mind away from the mosquito's burning bite.

Eventually, Pat made his way up the hill which led to Sally. Coming up to the gates, he realized that they'd be locked. He hadn't called ahead to let Sally know he was on his way.

He walked along the edge of the brick wall which surrounded Sally's residence. Groaning with effort, he clutched at the ivy growing along the wall. He didn't think if he'd be able to crawl over the obstacle, but he didn't know if he had any other option.

As if acknowledging that Pat had been forgiven, God provided.

When Pat came around the corner of the barrier, he saw a tall tree standing beside the brick wall. One of the boughs hung over the property.

Pat was really good at climbing trees. He had two favorites in the yard behind his own house. In fact, he'd been scuttling up one of those trees when the thought hit him: *I oughta ask Sally ta marry me.*

He'd been speaking to Sally for a long while now. He'd met her when he was a child and grew up confiding in her. When his momma was being strict, he went to Sally to complain. When his daddy was being rude, he went to Sally to cry. When he was happy, Sally was the first person he wanted to tell. When he was sad, he knew Sally wouldn't judge him.

If you don't marry her, someone else will. Pat had thought.

TOXIC

That thought scared him worse than thunder and lightning.

Pat knew *exactly* what it was people did when they got married. He could *hear* what married people did through the door leading into his momma and daddy's room. They squeaked, and grunted, and groaned—

And thinking of *someone else* making Sally make those noises upset Pat so much... he could've cried.

Sally was an angel, and Pat was certain that she had many suitors. He just needed to make sure that he was the first one to ask for her hand in marriage.

As he climbed the tree beside the brick wall, Pat imagined the wedding. He'd never been to one himself, but he'd seen them on the television.

He imagined Sally walking down the aisle, wearing white and smiling just as brightly as the sun.

Pat could picture his parents there too. After he came home with Sally, he was certain that his folks would forgive him for what he'd done. They'd understand that he had to do it, because he was in love... and men did foolish things when they were in love.

I'll apologize too. Mom'll forgive me. I know she will. If God can forgive me fer slappin' that moskeeter, then momma will definitely forgive me fer what I did.

He felt really bad about it still, and he reckoned he would continue to feel that way until he heard his mother say: "Oh, Pat. You know I can't stay mad at ya!"

Smiling, Pat shimmied along the length of the bough. He dangled his feet down, then dropped onto the ground. The fall from the tree to the earth was a bit higher than he expected. It sent a shockwave through his heels and up to his hips.

"Ouch!" Pat muttered, rubbing his hips with both hands. Frowning, he waddled toward Sally. He knew exactly where she was. She never moved.

"H-Hey, Sally. Ya see me drop outta that there tree?" He asked.

Sally didn't respond. That was the best thing about her. Unlike his momma or his daddy, Sally didn't talk over him. She also never called him names, like "bumpkin" or "stupid". She was so gentle and soft, she made him feel like he was swaddled in a cozy blanket when he was around her.

"S-Sally, I-I'd like ta talk ta ya to-today about s-something im-important. Jeepers. I'm st-stutter-stuttering a lot today, ain't I?" Pat knelt down in front of her. His body was slicked in sweat, and the mosquito lumps were itchy. He wanted to paw at them, but he was determined to tell her what she needed to hear.

"I-I wa-wanna ask ya something. Now, don't you laugh, cuz this is ser-serious. You won't laugh, will ya?"

Her silence was enough of a response for him. She was listening, and she was treating this with the necessary brevity. Confident that Sally was giving him her full attention, Pat pressed on. His tongue felt like it was weighed down in his mouth.

TOXIC

"I g-got ya this ring. Now, my momma... she didn't wanna give it up... so... so I hate ta tell ya this but... I-I had to ta-take it from her. I didn't w-wanna lie ta ya about that. I took it from her, b-but once momma see's this here ring sittin' pretty on yer finger, I'm *sure* she'll forgive me fer it!"

Pat pulled the ring from his pocket and allowed it to gleam in the sunlight.

His face flushed red.

He should've dipped the ring in the pond before coming over here.

The ring was stained with his momma's blood.

Maybe she won't notice...

Maybe she won't care...

Go on, Pat! Ask her!

Pat swallowed hard before saying: "W-will ya marry me, Sally? W-will ya be my wife?"

There was a moment of silence before Pat jumped up to his feet and pumped his fists in the air.

"Yippie!" He shouted in a high-pitched wail. "Oh, Sally! You have no idear how happy you done made me! Oh, thank you! Thank you, Sally! Thank ya!"

He knelt down once more, stuffing the ring back into his pocket. He wished he could slide it on Sally's finger right away, but good things took patience.

Pat pulled his tweed jacket open and reached into the pocket on the inner lining. He yanked out a spade he'd taken from his mother's garden. He knew stealing was wrong, but at least he hadn't had to chop off her fingers to steal *this* item from her.

Unlike the ring...

In his head, he recalled the way his poor momma had howled as he used her butcher's knife to cleave her fingers apart. She'd bled a great deal, spraying the kitchen walls and she danced with pain. A spark of guilt rushed through Pat, so he decided to focus on the present rather than the past.

"We'll get this ring on yer finger in no time, S-Sally!" Pat said. "Just gimme a few minutes. Then... we'll go back home and show momma and daddy just how good that ring looks on ya! He-He! Oh, S-Sally! You done made me tha happiest boy on Earth! I can't wait ta get married ta ya! And everyone will be there! You hear that, folks?" Pat glanced around the cemetery, smiling toward all his stony-faced friends. "Yer all invited!"

Quickly and happily, Pat drove the spade into the earth laid out ahead of Sally's grave. He didn't know how deep he'd have to dig to get to Sally's body, but if Pat was driven by anything, it was determination.

"I lo-love ya, Sally." Pat said as he scooped up a load of dirt and tossed it over his shoulder. "I love ya s-so much."

Cruising for Creeps

1957...

The car squealed up to the curb. A door popped open, and a greaser leaned out. He smelled musky, like hairspray and cigarette smoke. There was also the faint fragrance of beer underneath his off-putting aroma.

"Hey, baby! How about you jump in with us?" The greaser grinned, showing off his stained chompers.

Twyla crossed her arms and leaned on her hip. She was dressed nicely, but she was all alone. After the sock hop, she had a fight with her boyfriend, Hank. He wanted things to move a mite faster than she did. It seemed like all boys ever did was think about sex. That horrified Twyla. She didn't even want to *consider* opening her legs—like a hussy—until marriage. And even then, she was hoping her husband would understand if she needed some time before they did... the heavy stuff.

One look at the greaser and she could read his mind as good as any psychic. He was hounding for what she had cradled between her thighs.

"Get lost, creep!" She jabbed her finger in the air.

The greaser frowned. "C'mon, honey! I ain't gonna do nuthin' to ya. I just wanna ride around a bit, ya know? Get to know you and shit."

From the driver's seat, she heard another clown start laughing. She tried to peer into the car and catch sight of the trolls hanging out in there. She was surprised to realize that she recognized the driver. His name was Chet Holloway, and he wasn't too bad. He'd been her lab partner before, and he was actually pretty meek in person. But he dressed like a real tool, and he hung out with losers. They all wore the same leather jackets with an eagle stitched onto their backs.

"How many Eagles are in this coop, huh?" Twyla asked. "I see Chet... so that means you must be Nate!" She pointed to the greaser.

'My reputation proceeds me, huh?" Nate ran a hand through his oily hair, pushing it away from his smooth brow. He actually was a handsome boy; it was just a shame we wasted it on all that rock-and-roll nonsense. His hair was too long and shaggy, and he put mascara on his eyes.

It would definitely throw Hank into a fit if he caught me hanging out with these guys! Twyla thought with relish. *But it's not worth the risk. Who knows what these Neanderthals would do if I got in a car with 'em!*

"It's just the two of us in here." Chet said. He hefted himself halfway out the driver's side window and leaned his elbows against the roof of his car. "We've just been cruising today. Looking for some fun." He shrugged.

TOXIC

Chet was nimble, scrawny, and his face was riddled with acne. Nate could have been handsome if he cleaned himself up, but Chet was beyond help.

"Have y'all been to the sock hop? It's a hoot." Twyla countered.

"Yeah. That's kids' stuff!" Nate shucked his beefy shoulders. "We're out lookin' for some *real* fun!"

Nate glanced up and down the shopfronts. The street was busy with teens. Some were on their way to the sock hop while others were headed toward the end of the main street, where the drive-in sat.

Before their fight, Twyla and Hank had been keen to grab a milkshake and a burger at the drive in. But then, Hank had had to spoil it all by saying:

"Let's get it all to go and head on out to Willow's farm!"

Well! Twyla knew exactly what boys and girls did when they parked their cars by the fishing pond on Willow's farm. And she wanted nothing to do with it.

So, she'd told Hank that he could either enjoy her company at the drive-in parking lot, surrounded by lights, friends, and nosy teenagers... or he wouldn't be enjoying her company at all.

Hank had started acting like she'd kicked him in the crotch.

"You know, Twyla Maye, we've been going steady for a while now... and we ain't even so much as kissed? Why is that, huh? You ain't a lezzie, are ya?"

He claimed he'd only been joking after he saw her pout, but the damage was done. The salt had been rubbed into the wound. Twyla had marched away, turning a shoulder toward Hank's many protests and pleas.

Now, she was walking down main street on her own. All she carried with her was her purse, her pretty dress, and her dignity.

"Well, what is 'fun' for you two? Mailbox baseball?" Twyla asked.

Chet honked with laughter.

"Nah, you've got us all wrong, Ms. Twyla!" Nate said. "We're good boys."

"Yeah. Sure. And I'm the pope." Twyla cracked a welcoming smile, letting them know she was just fooling with them. *Maybe they ain't all bad. They've definitely got a better since of humor than most of my pals do. And I don't think they take themselves all that seriously. You'd have to be able to laugh at yourself if you went out in public looking like* that, *wouldn't you?*

"Seriously, though." Nate stepped out of the car, stood, and reached into the inner pocket of his creaky, leather jacket. He pulled out a carton of cigarettes. Twyla frowned at the distasteful tube while Nate plucked it from the box and popped it into his mouth. He lit his smoke with a flourish before continuing. "We aren't up to any trouble. In fact, we're out serving the public tonight."

"How so?" Twyla asked, intrigued.

"We're cruising for creeps." Nate said.

Twyla looked over the roof of the car and connected with Chet's eyes. She expected him to break into giggles, but his face had fallen. "Hey, Nate... you sure you oughta be tellin' her about—"

Nate pocketed his hands and allowed a gray cloud to slither through his teeth. "She's fine, Chet. I'm sure she'd understand exactly what it is if we explained it to her. In fact, we could use your help today, Twyla! If you wanna get involved, that is."

He whisked the cigarette out and tapped the ashes. Twyla watched them sprinkle the ground.

"W-what'd you say you were doing?" Twyla asked, a bit confused.

"We're cruising for creeps. You know... lookin' around for weirdos."

"I see two right now." Twyla tried to joke, but she was too flummoxed to pull the right tone.

Nate dropped his smoke before approaching her. "Listen, how about I buy you a shake and a burger and we'll explain it better to ya?"

Twyla smacked her lips. She was awful thirsty... and hungry. Her stomach burbled excitedly, betraying her.

"Well. I dunno. Hank might still be looking for me and—"

"My treat. And no funny business either." Nate raised his hands, as if she was arresting him. "I swear to Jesus."

She wanted to believe him, but she was suspicious. She didn't know Nate from Adam, but she did have something of an acquaintance with Chet. She glanced over at the skinny kid, and he gave her a reassuring smile.

"Scouts honor?" Twyla asked.

"I was never a scout, so it'd be a lie." Nate said.

"I respect your honesty. Okay, you buy me a burger and a shake... and tell me just what it is you two are up to tonight." Twyla confirmed.

"All right!" Nate opened the backdoor of his car.

Twyla shook her head. "No thanks. I'll walk. Besides, the drive-in is just down the street."

She walked ahead, and the car inched along the street beside her. Nate hung his head out the window like a dog and spoke to her while she sauntered.

She was thankful they'd respected her decision to stay out of their car. It boded well for their character.

"So, why ain't you and Hank together tonight?" Nate asked.

"Because Hank was getting fresh with me." Twyla said. "I'm a lady, after all."

"That you are." Nate said. "I'm sorry. I know I was jokin' around with you earlier but... if you want us to kick Hank's ass we'll do it."

"What a gesture." Twyla rolled her eyes and giggled. "You're funny, ya know? Maybe if you actually combed your hair, people wouldn't do *this* when you walked by." She exaggeratedly performed the sign of the cross, which made Nate chortle.

"Ha! Well, that's just rich comin' from you, square!"

"Who are you calling a square?" She cocked her hip and threw a lock of blonde hair over a slender shoulder.

TOXIC

Twyla was happy she'd run into the greasers. They were already picking up her spirits. Still, she hoped they wouldn't ruin things.

Boys had a tendency to do just that.

Boys like Hank.

Twyla realized she was biting the tip of her tongue. In her head, she replayed the argument with Hank. She supposed she'd been replaying it ever since she'd chosen to walk away from him. Half of her had expected Hank to pull up by the curb and invite her into his car so they could talk like adults and get over their spat. Instead, Chet and Nate had appeared, and they had made her giggle.

Or maybe they just see a vulnerable girl they can trick. Maybe it's all an act, and once they have your trust you'll be tied up in the trunk and carted out to Willow's farm anyways. And they aren't going to make out with you, Twyla. No... they'll make it with you! Whether you want it or not! And if you scream, not even God would hear yo—

What a ghastly thought! Twyla gulped down a boulder of saliva and tried to scrub her mind of its horrific wanderings. As she approached the drive-in diner on foot, Chet pulled ahead, found a spot, and parked. Nate was out in a flash. He strolled hurriedly to Twyla's side, as if he was worried that she'd be snatched away if he didn't reach her first.

"Whaddya like?" Nate asked. "Double cheese and extra pickles?"

"No pickles. Triple cheese." Twyla chirped.

TOXIC

She glanced around the parking lot. A busty carhop was standing by the window of a crowded car, jotting notes on a legal pad. Someone had turned their radio up, and a rock band was crooning over the airwaves.

Inside the restaurant, Twyla saw a lot of kids her age.

She wondered if she was soiling her reputation, going out for dinner with two "hoods" like Chet and Nate. There was a saucy appeal to the prospect. If word got back to Hank that his girl was spending her time with greasers instead of him, he'd be mortified!

He'd probably feel emasculated too.

She can't get nothing good off Hank, so she hangs out with hoodlums instead! Hah!

She wagered that no one else but her was thinking too deeply about any of this stuff. But the only way Twyla thought she'd slow her brain down was if she took a hammer to it, so she let her theories run like loosened bunnies in a pasture.

They walked into the dine-in and found a booth. Respectably, Nate and Chet sat across from Twyla, so she wasn't squeezed between a glass wall and a musky boy. When a waitress came over, Nate did the ordering. A triple cheese burger for Twyla, an order of chili fries for himself, and a regular burger for Chet.

"Milkshakes!" Twyla proclaimed before the waitress could zip away. "I'd like chocolate!"

"Me too!" Chet added.

"I'm good. Just a Coke." Nate said.

When the waitress left, the threesome sat in uneasy silence. Then, Twyla leaned onto her elbows and addressed the boys frankly.

"What did you mean by 'cruising for creeps'?"

Again, Chet looked nervous.

He glanced over his shoulder, as if he expected the couple in the neighboring booth to have heard Twyla's question.

"It's just something we like to do." Nate said with a shrug. "You know, we think of it as a public service."

"But what is it?" Twyla asked. "A game?"

Nate leaned forward and spoke in a dull whisper. Twyla had to turn her head just to hear him.

"We go out... we find a creep... and we bust him up."

Twyla chuckled.

She was surprised to see that both Nate and Chet were wearing grim expressions. They were absolutely serious about this.

"Wait—what?" Twyla screwed up her brows. "You do what?"

"It's like Nate said." Chet coughed. "We pick out a creep, go find him, and give him a bit of what he deserves, ya' know?"

"No. I don't." Twyla said. "So... tell me what you mean."

Nate cleared his throat. "Y-you remember what happened to Billy Fincher?"

She did. Two months ago, a student had been found tied to a tree with his pants and underwear removed. His head was hidden behind a paper bag.

TOXIC

The word "rapist" had been written in bold lettering along the face of his mask. Beneath the bag, Billy had had a sock shoved into his mouth, and a layer of duct tape placed over the orifice, preventing him from screaming for help. From what Twyla had heard, Billy had had one of his ribs broken early on, and he was left to suffer in agony until he was discovered the next evening by a family out for a picnic at the public park.

"Yeah. I remember." Twyla confirmed with a shudder. "Do you guys... did you..."

Chet nodded solemnly.

"W-what? Why?" Twyla almost shouted.

Chet and Nate shushed her, glancing conspiratorially around the restaurant.

The waitress came around with a platter of food. After she left, Twyla stared glumly at her burger. She didn't know if she'd be able to take a single bite. She hadn't *seen* what had happened to Billy but hearing about it had been traumatizing enough.

Chet spoke first, filling her in on the story.

"It happened awhile back. We were hanging out on the stoop, smoking and chatting, when this little girl came up to us. She must've been—what? —nine or ten. Cute little pigtails. Reminded me of my little cousin.

"She came up to us and asked, 'are you the toughest guys in town?' Well, we thought it was all a joke so of course we said we were, and that we'd mop the floor with anyone who even looked at us cross-eyed. She took out this purse she had on her and pulled out a wad of bills. She held them out at arms-length, and I could see she was holding back tears." Chet's voice tapered off.

Nate held his breath. He took a fry and shoved it in his mouth, then he took a long sip of his soda. After he had wet his dry mouth, he continued the story for Chet. "Anyways, we knew something was off. She wasn't like... pulling our legs. She started cracking up, and we decided to take her seriously. She told us that Billy Fincher was her babysitter, and he'd been... doing stuff to her. Ever since she was little, he'd always come over to take care of her. You know, since he lived across the street. Her parents didn't think nothing about a teen boy looking after a little kid. They... they didn't know what he was doing to her."

Twyla wasn't sure she could conceive of what they were telling her either. What indeed did a teenage boy see in a small child? It took a twisted mind to even consider such horrors.

It was decided for Twyla then. She pushed her burger aside.

Nate continued in a whisper. "Well, we got pretty riled. She said she'd pay us to keep her safe, because he was going to come over and babysit again that weekend. We told her to keep the money. Told her... we'd take care of it."

"So, we went out together that Friday. We found him where he usually hangs on weekends when he wasn't babysitting... the pool hall. We played him for a bit, convinced him that he was a cool guy and we just wanted to hang with him. Then, Nate told him we had some beer stowed away in the creek that runs through the park."

Nate spoke next. "When we got him in the park, we used a tire iron to crack his ribs. While he was crying, we tied him up to the tree and put the bag over his head. Then, we told him we knew what he'd been up to... and if he told, so would we. We expected him to tell, but we didn't care. Not when he was... *hurting* that young girl. In fact, I kind of hoped he'd tell."

"But he didn't. As far as the cops know, he was jumped by some thugs. And no... he didn't see what they looked like." Chet snorted.

"A few weeks later, the gal came back during recess and told us she had a new babysitter, and Billy wouldn't even look at her house when he walked by. Twyla, lemme tell ya... it was worth it just seeing the smile on that girl's face." Nate's eyes seemed to swim with tears. Self-consciously, he pulled a napkin from the compartment and dabbed at his eyes.

"So, we decided to do it again." Chet said.

"Y-you went after Billy a second time?" Twyla asked, aghast.

Chet shook his head. "No. No. We think Billy's learned his lesson. But, going through all *that*... it made us aware of a few things about this town. It's full of creeps, you know? It's just that no one likes to talk about it. They'd rather we all wore smiles and pretended everything was hunky-dory. But there's something slimy beneath this place."

"So, we started paying attention." Nate said.

"Yeah. We... started looking." Chet scratched his chin. "So, here's where you come in, Twyla. Because... we didn't just stumble onto you tonight."

Twyla felt her heart clinch up in her chest. Both of these boys had just confessed to committing a crime. Even though she found it justifiable, it was still a crime. And now, they were admitting that she somehow fit into the next crime that they intended to commit.

"We... we were following Hank tonight. And when you walked away from him, we decided that you needed to know." Chet swallowed a lump. "You need to know about the monster you're dating."

Twyla released a dry chuckle. "What are you talking about?"

Chet and Nat shared a glance. Then, Chet reached into his leather jacket and pulled out an envelope. He passed it across the table, then tapped it with a spindly finger. "What's inside here is a story, Twyla. It was a story written by a girl from your class. She didn't want anyone knowing who she was, so I copied it so her handwriting couldn't be traced back to her. The original—er—confession has been burned."

"A few people found out about what we did to Billy, and why. Little girls don't keep secrets very well. For now, our services are just a rumor." Nate explained. "But... a few people recognize the good in what we did. This girl approached us a week ago and... told us about Hank. Now, Twyla... I gotta warn ya. It's bad. It's really bad. When you read this, it'll do more than just change the way you see Hank. It'll make you lose faith in God."

Twyla had to read it now that Nate had made such a spectacular proclamation.

She took the envelope and peeled it open, tearing out the letter and observing its informal hand. Chet wasn't much of a calligraphist. His words were mushed together, seeping into the boundaries of their neighbors.

Twyla read, and as she did her eyes grew bigger... and bigger... and bigger...

She looked up at her newfound friends after finishing. She felt breathless, terrified, and hurt. It was as if Hank had performed those awful deeds onto her, rather than the poor girl he'd liquored up at a party Twyla hadn't even been privy to.

The pregnant girl, who'd been keeping her baby a secret...

A secret from everyone but the father...

...*Hank*.

She'd woken up to find him pushing a coat hanger into her womb. She'd screamed, but he'd tied her down to the table in his woodshed and she had no hopes of fighting him off.

She'd cried as pieces of her child were ripped from her uterus and scattered across the floor.

But there was viler than the nonconsensual abortion. The worst part was what he did with the scraps.

I'll never forget it for as long as I'll live. And if I die, it will be because I relived this moment one

TOXIC

time too many at midnight, when the memory feels its freshest, Hank Watson pushed my baby's tissue into my mouth. He sealed it closed with his hand before telling me to swallow. I cried and pleaded, but eventually... I did what he wanted. I always did what Hank wanted. All his girls did. I wonder if they were forced to eat their unborn babies too. I wonder if they were made to atone for his sins. Anyways, he didn't stop until every shred of my child was swallowed, and he didn't untie me until after he'd gone off to shower and nap. I was left in his woodshed, desperate and begging. When he let me go, he made it clear that if I told... I'd be revealing the things we'd done. I'd reveal to my parents and friends that I was a slut who fucked out of wedlock, and that my punishment would be worse than his. I believe him. I truly do. So... I don't want him to be hurt and shamed. No. I want you to kill Hank Watson, so he never does to another girl the things he did to me.

"I... I don't believe it." Twyla shook her head. Tears dribbled down her cheeks and landed in her lap. She rifled through the papers, which described how Hank had wooed this unnamed girl. He had convinced her that he was breaking up with his current girlfriend, and he only had eyes for her. He'd told her he'd marry her after she revealed she was pregnant. Then... then..

Then he'd forcibly aborted the child before feeding it to its suffering mother.

"I do." Chet said. "You didn't see the expression on her face. It looked like something had *broken* inside her."

"Why are you doing this to me?" Twyla snapped, struggling to keep her tone under control. She didn't want anyone in the diner to realize that she was distressed. Using the backs of her hands, she smeared tears across her face.

"We didn't think it would be right to... do what we plan on doing without letting you know about it." Chet said. "If he got killed and you didn't know, then you'd have mourned him."

"So, you plan on doing it? You're going to kill my boyfriend? Just because someone told a story about him. You guys are crazy. I'll—I'll tell the cops. *I'll scream if you touch me!*" She shouted as Chet reached out for her. He recoiled, holding his hand as if she'd burned it.

"Calm down, Twyla." Nate rasped, taking a look around the diner.

"So, what do you expect me to do?" Twyla asked. "You expect me to just sit back and let you—" She couldn't finish her sentence. Her teeth started to chatter, as if an icicle was being drawn up the ridges of her spine.

"We want you to help us." Nate said. "We want you to help us kill the bastard. Or... we want you to rest assured that you didn't have to spend the rest of your life with him."

"You don't have to help If you don't want to, but we didn't want you thinking that the world was being unfair to you. This is justice, Twyla. What he did to that girl—"

"Who is she?" Twyla interjected. "You have to tell me."

Chet and Nate both shook their heads. "She didn't want anyone to know. That's part of our gig. Total secrecy." Nate said.

"How many people have you killed?" Twyla asked.

Nate swallowed. "This'll be the first."

"We've taken care of a lot of creeps though. We broke Joey Spindler's nose. We're the reason Pastor John Fairchild came to church in crutches last week. We—we've been cleaning this city up. One creep at a time." Chet said.

"Like Batman and Robin."

"Only, we can't figure out who's Batman and who's Robin." Chet rolled his eyes.

"I'm obviously Batman."

"Yeah, but you don't drive."

"It's a junker, not the Batmobile." Nate picked up his soda and took a long gulp.

"You're crazy. Both of you." Twyla said. "I oughta scream. Let everyone know exactly what you two have been up to, and what you plan on doing. I oughta!"

"Yeah. But... will you?" Nate furrowed his brow.

There was a pregnant pause. The three teens all looked at each other, as if in a standoff. Twyla's lips trembled and she tucked her chin into her neck.

"Because now... you're looking back at all your memories with Hank, aren't you? Are you remembering anything about him that makes you believe this story? I bet you are." Nate leaned in. "Has he ever gotten angry with you, Twyla?"

Twyla shook her head, but she recalled the fight that had built up to this conversation. He'd been so lecherous. It crept through like a rat peeking out from a hole in a wall. She'd seen a dark twinkle in his eye that told her that all he saw when he looked at her... was meat. She was no better than a T-Bone steak in his eyes—

—but that just meant he was a *boy*, not that he was a... a *monster*!

Had he gotten mad at her before? She tried to picture Hank as the woman abusing piece of shit that Nate and Chet portrayed him as.

"We need to ask him." Twyla said.

"Huh?" Chet asked.

"If we catch him, we'll ask him if he did it or not. I'll be able to tell if he's lying. Maybe he'll even have an alibi for that night. We just need to ask him first, and you have to promise me that we'll let him go if he's innocent, okay?" Twyla stammered. "If he... if he lies to me... I'll let you do what you have to do."

"Twyla, he's been lying to you the whole time." Nate stated.

"No, he hasn't. Because all we talk about is football, and college, and rock music. We've never talked about... anything real, so he's never had the chance to lie about his feelings. Trust me. I'll know if he did it or not. I just need to hear from him

TOXIC

first." Twyla said. "And that's that. We don't do this if you don't at least allow him a trial."

Chet snorted.

Nate nodded. "Okay. We'll do it your way. But... I'm not going to disappoint the girl he hurt."

"What do you mean? You'll kill him anyways?"

"No. I mean, I'm putting him in the hospital tonight, no matter what. Which department depends on your call." Nate said. "But I reckon he'll be mighty comfy in the morgue."

×

Driving through the streets of their little community, Twyla looked out the foggy window and watched as other cars bustled around them. They could hear loud tunes and even louder laughs rising from each car they passed.

But Twyla didn't feel like laughing.

Sitting in the passenger seat of the Batmobile, she tried her best not to make eye-contact with her chaperones. Nate and Chet were smoking and chatting, but they were merely trying to fill the air with something other than tension.

Eventually, Chet fiddled with the radio and *Dream Lover* seeped into the car. Bobby Darin's smooth voice usually gave Twyla the sweats, but she couldn't stand his crooning now. She stared hard at the sidewalk, looking for her beau.

Hank was probably in his own car, but there was a chance he was walking. He was definitely going to be on the lookout for his girl, she reasoned. After their little quarrel, he'd be looking to kiss and make up.

"My house." She suddenly said. "He'll be at my house."

"You sure?" Chet asked.

"Yep. Last time we fought, he threw pebbles at my window. I'll bet my bottom dollar he's there now."

They drove away from town and toward the suburbs. Twyla led the way, giving Chet directions. She was thankful that the two didn't already know where she lived. It wouldn't have surprised her, but it definitely would've frightened her.

What if it's all a trick? Twyla thought. *What if they do this every week for shits and giggles. They pick up a gal and make her believe terrible things about her boyfriend, just to see how she reacts. They could be sadists, Twyla. You don't know them as well as you know Hank... yet they now have you convinced that Hank is—*

"It's toward the end of this cul-de-sac." Twyla said. "Park here at the corner and I'll go ahead. If we pull up together then he'll know something is up."

"Seems fair." Chet said, braking hard before he could turn the corner. "I'll follow behind, just to make sure you're safe."

"I'll be fine."

"You don't know that. Remember, the girl he hurt trusted him too." Chet said. "I'll stick to the backyards. Don' worry. He won't spot me."

Twyla sighed. She didn't really suppose she had much of a choice when it came to the semantics of their operation.

She threw the door open and stepped out slowly.

If they were sadists, they wouldn't have let you leave the car. They'd have hurt you already, wouldn't they?

God.

Why did this have to happen to me?

Twyla felt guilty. None of this had happened to *her*. It had happened to the anonymous woman. She closed her eyes and tried to picture the pain the poor girl had endured.

Shaking her head, Twyla walked up the street and toward her house. Her parents were gone for the weekend—a fact Hank was aware of—so she wasn't astonished to see him sitting on the stoop that lead to the front door.

Hank perked up like a famished pooch. His saucer-shaped ears seemed to rise by the sides of his head. His red hair was bright orange in the pale porch light. His freckles looked like spots of blood. He was wearing his letter-jacket, and a pair of tight jeans.

Hank lurched up to his feet and dashed toward her. Twyla almost leapt away, afraid that he was going to tackle her. She glanced toward the shadowy yards leading up to her house. Chet would rush out if she was in danger, wouldn't he?

Hank slowed down a few yards away from her. He skidded to a stop, then he held his arms out. "Twyla, I'm so sorry. I—I can't believe I was so terrible to you today." He looked as if he'd been weeping.

Twyla's heart broke for him, as it had been trained to do whenever he cried. She didn't know if she could trust her heart in these moments, but she trusted her brain even less. It was like a teeter-totter, tilting back and forth between loving Hank and being afraid of him.

Hank slowed when he realized that Twyla wasn't falling into his embrace. Awkwardly, he let his arms dangle by his sides.

"Are you... mad at me?" He sounded so meek and worried.

"I... I don't know, Hank. Maybe I just need time before I let you touch me again." Twyla whispered, taking another glance into the yard beside her. Was that Chet in the shadows? Was he slinking toward them?

"I'm... I didn't hurt you." Hank protested, and she saw a flicker of anger buried in his gaze.

"You did." Twyla said.

"I mean, not physically."

"No. But... I don't know, Hank. Tonight, was a wash. Let's call it what it is. You wanted to go necking and I didn't."

"But... you never want to do *anything*."

"I want to do plenty. Just not that! I'm not ready. Can't you just accept that?" Twyla shuddered. This wasn't a *real* argument for her. She kept imagining what it would feel like to have a coat hanger shoved into her privates.

She wondered if it had torn that poor girl's womb open, preventing her from ever carrying another child again.

"No. I mean, you're my girlfriend!" Hank shrugged. "You're... we're supposed to be a couple, you know? And that means we need to take care of each other. I've been taking care of you, right? You feel safe with me, right?"

"Y-yes."

"Then why won't you just spend time with me? We didn't have to go to Willow's Farm if that's what you were worried about. We could—I mean— we could go anywhere where you'd feel safe with me—"

"It's not a big deal." Twyla said. 'I just..." She sighed exaggeratedly. "Can we take a walk, Hank?"

Her boyfriend nodded slowly. "Yeah. We can take a walk."

Twyla turned and waited for Hank to stroll up to her side. He lashed an arm over her shoulder. She could feel the tension in his muscles.

Together, they walked down the shaft of the cul-de-sac, making their way to the corner. She hoped Nate had turned the car off. If the lights were on, Hank would direct her away from the corner and take her away from Chet and Nate.

She was relieved when they turned the bend, and she saw that the car was emptied. Nate had snuck out as well.

They're keeping an eye on us. Like wardens. Like parents.

TOXIC

God, what if they are wrong? What if this girl tricked them because she was jealous of me? Maybe she had a crush of Hank, and decided that if she can't have him... neither can I.

That's stupid.

No one would make up such a grotesque story.

"What's on your mind, Twyla?" Hank said. "What are you thinking?"

Twyla bit into the tip of her tongue. Her teeth slid into the muscle too easily. She felt blood slip down her throat and stain the insides of her cheeks.

What was on her mind? What was she thinking? The answer was simple. She was imagining what it felt like to swallow strips of tissue that had been dug out of her uterus—

"A lot." She said.

"Well, tell me about it. I'm here for you, darling." Hank reached over and tipped her chin up. She flinched, involuntarily.

"What?" Hank asked, his voice cross. "What's going on with you, Twyla?" He alleviated his arm from her shoulder and crossed it over his chest. He looked like a pouting infant. "What's so wrong with me that we can't even have us a conversation, huh?"

Ask him about it. Ask him about it, Twyla. Otherwise, it'll eat you up inside. Like a cancer. You have to ask him about what he did.

Listening to the voice in her head, Twyla spoke before she could second guess herself. "Do you have other girlfriends, Hank?"

Hank froze.

TOXIC

He should've just said "no", right? What's taking him so long?

He's probably just surprised by the question.

"I—I'd understand if you did." Twyla said. "I know you haven't been getting... what you need from me."

Where had *that* come from? It was an outright lie, but Twyla theorized that he'd be more truthful if she seemed accepting of it.

Hank pocketed his hands and sighed deeply. "None of them have been serious."

Twyla almost broke into sobs. She batted her lashes, pulling back tears.

"Oh. Anyone I'd know?" Twyla asked, trying to sound as casual as she could.

"No. They never really swam in our circles. Jeez, Twyla. I'm awfully sorry. If you want me to leave then I'll—"

"No. I told you it was all right, and it is. I know you're a man and that men have—well—needs. Just tell me this, so I can sleep better at night. You haven't gotten any of these gals pregnant, have you?"

"Sheesh, Twyla!" Hank shrugged. "I can't believe we're even talking about this! Are you sure you aren't mad? Because by golly, you have every right to be." His childlike tone was infuriating now. He was acting like he'd been caught with his hand in a cookie jar. Pressing through her whirlwind of negative emotions, Twyla gave Hank a half-convincing smile.

"Honestly, it takes the pressure off my shoulders. I want you to be happy Hank, and I don't want to be the reason why you... aren't. I can wait until marriage, but if you can't then—well—I just hope you're being 'safe;. So, have you gotten anyone pregnant?" Twyla asked, trying not to let her ulterior motives slip through her words. More blood oozed out of her tongue. She wondered if it had stained her teeth crimson. Had her smile been a ghoulish one?

"No." Hank said. "No. I haven't."

Twyla could have sighed with relief. He sounded truthful. Which meant that the story she'd been handed was a lie. She definitely agreed that Hank should wind up in the hospital for his infidelity, but she was relieved that he wouldn't be dying tonight—

"Well..." Hank trailed off.

'What?" Twyla asked after the silence became unbearable.

"We had a scare but... we took care of it. She's not pregnant. You don't need to worry."

Images played through Twyla's head. She pictured a drunk girl waking up in a woodshed, tied down to a work table. Naked below the waist. The woman cried and screamed as Hank rootled around in her chambers with a rusty hanger. Twyla saw a gush of tissue, and she watched as Hank gathered it up in his hands and forced it into her—

Twyla spun around, knelt, and vomited.

Yellow bile spewed forth from her gullet and spattered across the dewy lawn beside her. Hank was quick to grab her hair and pull it away from her face, but she wished his hands would leave her. She knew what those hands had done, and she didn't want them anywhere near her body.

Coughing harshly, she battered his hands away. When she sucked in a breath between waves of upchuck, a strand of hair drifted into her mouth and triggered another gagging cough.

"Jeez, Twyla!" Hank shouted. "I thought you said you were okay with everything!"

Twyla looked up at the yard with blurry eyes. She spotted two lumps growing out from the shadows beneath a thick oak tree. They walked slowly and steadily, careful not to alert Hank to their presence.

Twyla pulled her hair from her mouth and wiped her face with the heel of her hand. Her skin felt sticky, and her breath was acidic. The sudden expulsion of puke had hurt her throat, and she felt it *click* when she swallowed.

"What's wrong, Twyla?" Hank asked, desperation is his voice. 'Don't be like this. You said it was okay! You said—Hey. Hey! Get lost!"

Twyla looked up again, noting that Nate and Chet were now standing side-by-side at the edge of the yard. They were only a few feet away from the couple.

Hank stepped in front of Twyla, as if he was her protector.

"The lady doesn't look too good." Nate said. "In fact, she looks pretty upset. You do something to upset her, buddy-boy?" Nate's tone was a shrewd mix of menacing and jovial, as if he'd say he was "just kidding" if Hank took him too seriously.

Twyla imagined a spider laying a trap for a fly.

Hank tightened his hands into fists. He recognized the covert hostility. "None of your business, greaser."

"You know what I can't stand, Hank?" Nate stepped forward. "I can't stand watching men like you hurt on women. It makes my blood run cold."

"I ain't hurtin' her. Now scram, before I call the cops!"

"I don't think you'll wanna do that." Chet spoke up. "I think you'll wanna shut the fuck up for once and let us do the talking."

Twyla lashed out. Catching Hank by surprise, she tackled his legs and sent him sprawling. She heard his body *splat* against the pool of vomit she'd left on the yard's edge.

Before Hank could scream, Chet had turned him over and put a hand over his mouth. Hank's eyes bugged out of his skull as the boy's hefted him up by his arms and dragged him across the road and back toward their car. He stared at Twyla, confused, hurt, and betrayed.

Twyla followed close behind, knitting her fingers together and chewing on her tongue.

Chet got the trunk open. Together, the greasers lugged Hank into it.

When Chet slammed the door, Hank reached out for the lip of the trunk. Twyla watched in horror as the lid thumped into his digits. There was a *crunch* as all four of Hank's outstretched fingers broke.

TOXIC

He yowled like an alley-cat.

"Shit." Chet muttered. He pulled the trunk up and callously tossed the busted hand into the darkness before he banged the lid back in place.

Nate and Chet turned around and crossed their arms, like sentinels.

"You okay, Twyla?" Nate asked.

Twyla nodded, then she shook her head "no".

"You wanna go home and catch some rest?" Nate asked. "We can handle it from here."

"No." Twyla said. "No. I... I need to be there. He did it. He did it. And he needs to be punished for it."

"I'm sorry." Chet said. "I know this is a lot but— shut up!" He turned and beat his fist against the trunk. Hank's objections were muted, but they hadn't let up since he'd been sealed away.

"Let's hurry up." Twyla walked around the car and flung the passenger door open. "Now. Before someone sees us."

Twyla realized she had no idea where they were going by the time the Batmobile had coasted out of town. She was too focused on the noise Hank was making in the trunk. Inside the car, his screams and pleas were amplified.

"You hurt my hand! You really hurt my fuckin' hand! Please! Lemme go!"

"Shut up!" Nate said from the backseat.

"Aw, let him shout." Chet said from behind the wheel. "It'll wear him out by the time we get there."

"W-where are we going?" Twyla asked.

"Somewhere where we won't be bothered." Chet said stoically.

When the car ambled down the gravel road that led to Willow's farm, Twyla had to snicker at the irony. No matter what she did, her night had ended here—at this place where Hank was going to take her, if she hadn't had the nerve to stand up for herself.

She turned her head and caught Chet watching her from the side. He coughed and glanced back at the road.

"Are we really going to kill him?" Twyla asked.

"We are." Chet said.

"Good."

Chet pulled the car to the side of the gravel road. Around them, the trees were thick and dark. They were skeletal, and their limbs ended in twisted daggers. The trees no longer looked elegant and beautiful, as she remembered them. They looked like weapons.

Everything had changed for Twyla, just as it had changed for Nate and Chet when they started this business.

The world is violent, and cruel, and vile. But it wears a smile. It tricks you into thinking it loves you, then it stabs you in the fucking back.

Twyla blinked away a new rush of sobs.

She threw the door open and climbed out of the car.

Chet followed, then circled around the car and threw the trunk lid open.

TOXIC

There was a *pop*, which reminded Twyla of a rock plopping into a stagnant pond.

Chet stumbled back, holding his throat with both hands.

"What happened?" Nate asked as he wiggled loose from the back seat. "What was that?"

There was another *pop*.

Twyla screamed.

Chet's head snapped back as the bullet smacked into his brow, poking a black hole above and between his eyebrows.

"Chet!" Nate shouted.

Chet's hands dropped, exposing the first wound that had been plugged through his throat. The bullet had punctured his Adam's apple. Blood jettisoned from the wound, spraying the trunk and washing the back windshield of the car.

"Mother... fucker." Chet sputtered before falling onto his back. He lay on the gravel with his arms and legs spread. Blood gurgled from both holes, like a crimson fountain.

Hank struggled loose from the trunk. He kept his broken hand tucked beneath his arm-pit. His other hand held a six-shooter. A miniature pistol, which Hank's father had given him for his seventeenth birthday.

He's had that all night. Twyla thought. *He would have used it on Nate and Chet earlier... but he didn't want to fire blindly while the car was moving. He waited... for the right moment.*

"What the fuck?" Nate asked, his mouth hanging loose.

"Yeah. What the fuck?" Hank sneered before firing his gun once more.

The bullet smashed through Nate's lower jaw. Twyla heard the bones jangle apart like cracked clay. An explosion of blood stippled her face. The liquid was so warm, she thought she'd been lit on fire.

Twyla reeled backward, pedaling her arms with panic.

Nate fell to his knees. Both of his hands went to his decimated jaw. Gore slipped between his fingers in knotted ropes. He coughed, and she could hear his divided jaw *clatter* with the motion.

Nate began to make sounds that reminded Twyla of a baby's mewls.

"Stupid fucks!" Hank wandered over to Nate. "You really thought you were doing something, huh? Well *fuck you*!"

Hank forced the nozzle of his pistol against Nate's left eye. Nate began to hyperventilate, but he was too surprised and hurt to defend himself.

When the gun went off, its bark was muffled by the moist eruption of eyeball fluid and brain matter. Twyla watched as the back of Nate's head blew apart. Smoking bone chips and streamlets of tissue fell out from the hole, smattering across the road like an abstract painting.

Nate tipped back and lay in a heap on the ground.

Hank sighed, then used his sleeve to wipe the blood away from his face. His hand hung lopsidedly, cradling his weapon. He looked up toward Twyla, blinking slowly.

"Y'all fucked up my hand." He said, holding out his injured limb. "Would ya look at this? Totally fucked. God. I've got a game on Friday, you stupid bitch! You just ruined my fucking career!"

Twyla's lips trembled. She felt like vomiting once again.

"All over some bitch." Hank sneered. "What'd she do? Huh? Tell you what a monster I am? Tell you how I made her eat her *sin*? Well, fuck you! It's what she deserved!"

He held the gun up and pulled the trigger. Twyla felt a blurt of pain, then a rush of warm fear swaddled her. She stumbled back, clutching at her belly, where the bullet had skewered her. Blood oozed out from the wound, quilting her skirt and dribbling against the ground.

Oh. Oh. I've been shot.

That wasn't supposed to happen.

Shit.

"You know the worst part of it, Twyla?" Hank asked, speaking through his teeth. "The worst part is... I really thought you'd be my girl."

Hank held up the gun once more.

Six shots. Two for Chet, two for Nate... and now, two for me. Twyla thought.

Hank fired.

Twyla juked down. Bending her stomach caused a flair of pain to scorch through her. It was as if a hot iron had been plunged into her gut, and it was being cranked with her movements. She felt as if a bowling ball was sitting on her bowels. She pushed through the pain and barreled forward.

TOXIC

She rammed her head into Hank's pelvis. It was the closest she'd ever been to his crotch. She could feel his genitals mash against her skull as she bore down onto him with all her weight. Hank tumbled back and landed on the ground. He scrabbled rearward, shrieking as he accidentally put pressure on his broken hand.

Fighting through tears and agony, Twyla followed him, clutching at his bile and blood greased cloths. She dragged him onto his back, then straddled him.

"Wait!" Hank shouted. "Hold on! Stop!"

Twyla roared as she grabbed him by his floppy ears. She pulled hard, drawing his skull up. Then, she slammed his head hard against the gravel ground. She heard something break and watched as blood piped out behind him.

"Oh, god!" Hank's eyes turned huge.

When she lifted his head again, she saw that she'd smashed his skull into an uprooted stone. The craggy rock ended in a twisted nub, which was blunt enough to remind her of an upraised finger.

Twyla dropped Hank's head.

Slowly, she wriggled off of him. Keeping her eyes on Hank, she stood and braced herself against the opened passenger door.

Hank was weeping like a child. With his good hand, he reached behind his skull. He brought the palm back and gawped at the glittery blood that filled it. Whining like a puppy with its tail stuck in a doorjamb, Hank looked up at Twyla and held his hand out for her to observe.

"L-look what y-you did to me." His chin crumpled and snot began to spill out from his nostrils.

Twyla was too stunned to speak. Her night had descended into chaos and bloodshed, and the fact that she'd caused so much hurt—even if it was in self-defense—was baffling to her overstressed mind.

This is only a fraction of the agony that the unfortunate girl felt.

Twyla held her aching stomach. She wondered if there was now a painful connection between her and the girl, beyond the fact that they'd dated the same demon.

Both of our wombs have been destroyed by him. Different methods... same results.

Twyla coughed.

A shipment of blood fell from her mouth and stained the already soused ground beneath her.

The pain was turning cold.

Hank snickered. "G-got you pretty good... too."

Twyla coughed again. Blood poured down her chin. She felt as if she was exhaling hot pennies.

"Y-you didn't have to do this." Hank muttered, rolling over onto his side. He clutched his ruined hand to his chest. Each finger was pointed a different direction. "We could've just... gone back to the hop."

"You're a real piece of shit, Hank." Twyla seethed.

"I did it for you." Hank muttered. "Believe it or not... I did it for you."

Twyla was aghast. There was no way he actually meant that.

She could feel her heart beating between her ears.

"I didn't want her to... to tell anyone about the baby. I knew it would've... would've embarrassed you so much."

Twyla shook her head. "Fuck you."

Hank coughed. Strands of blood sprayed across the gravel. "I love you, Twyla. I love you."

Twyla stumbled toward him. She reached down and grabbed him by the collar of his shirt. He fidgeted and moaned, but all of his fight had leaked out of him.

Twyla pulled Hank toward the car, grunting with exertion as she went. Her veins were freezing over, and she could feel feces crawling down her legs. She couldn't care about her body shutting down, all she wanted to do was insure that Hank suffered right before he died.

She laid his head down in the jamb on the passenger side of the door.

"No. Twyla, stop!"

She took the door in both of her hands and slammed it hard. She heard a wet *smack* as Hank's head was caught between the door and the frame. He moaned loudly, like a bleating goat.

Twyla pulled the door back, then rammed it closed again. It jumped in her hands, bouncing as it connected with Hank's cranium. She could see a crevice forming along the top of his skull, splitting his head down the middle. The red gorge sprayed blood in separate directions.

Hank began to jitter spasmodically, as if his nerves were being electrocuted.

"Fuck... you!" Twyla bellowed as she slammed the door for the final time.

There was an immediate and violent eruption of blood. Wormy strands of brain matter wriggled loose from the cleft through the top of Hank's dome. His body fell limp and his head slipped out from its spot on the door's frame. Blood sloshed across the gravel, trickling like a babbling brook.

Twyla wasn't finished. She straddled his back and dug her fingers into the fissure. Screaming with effort, she pulled on the skull until it cracked in half like a meaty walnut.

Twyla fell back and kicked herself away from Hank's corpse. Her hands were gloved in gore, and her vision had been tinted red. Her thoughts began to swim, split, and fragment in her head. She smelled her own sickness, Hank's bodily discharges, and something smoky.

Before she fell unconscious, Twyla could hear a car grinding to a stop nearby.

They... found... you... found you... found you... some... one... found... you...

Her breath hitched and her eyes went black—

×

Twyla didn't believe she had survived.

When she woke up a week later, she believed she would be led to the pearly gates by an escort, and she'd be judged for the things she had done. But instead, she was attended to by nurses, doctors, and her wailing parents.

Her folks had rushed home after getting the call that Twyla had been involved in some sort of accident out on the road that led to Willow's Farm. The old farmer had been drawn out of his home by the sounds of gunfire. When he found the half-dead girl and the threesome of corpses, he'd gathered her up and taken her to town.

When word got out that Twyla had woken up from her coma, the old farmer came by to give her flowers and wish her well.

She'd broken into hysterical tears upon seeing him. He reminded her too much of the things that had happened in the backwoods that night. The events that should have killed her...

The police talked to her. It was obvious that they couldn't believe the story she told them, especially since she couldn't give them the name of the woman that Hank had allegedly abused.

What saved her was Hank's pistol. The weapon was found on the scene, and the bullets used on Nate, Chet, and Twyla had been linked back to the supply Hank kept in his bedroom. The gun was clearly his, and it had been fired by him... and so, Twyla's actions were deemed an act of self-defense.

×

Twyla was reading a book for school when the girl walked into her hospital room. She looked up from *Of Mice and Men* and offered the stranger a smile. Plenty of people from school swung by the hospital during visiting hours to check on Twyla. As she understood it, she'd become something of a legend among her classmates. She could only imagine how tall the tales had become.

TOXIC

"Hi." The girl said, giving Twyla a thin smile. She was mousy, bespectacled, and her clothes were beige. She looked as if she was attempting to blend in with the walls. "Hi, Twyla." The girl tried to speak at a louder register, but her throat seemed to combat her efforts.

"Hi." Twyla closed her book.

The two stared at each other in silence for a moment. Twyla wondered if she should break the unease with a joke, but her brain had been moving sluggishly ever since she'd been shot. Even reading a book as small as the Steinbeck paperback had become a mountainous challenge. She kept restarting sentences and losing track of characters.

"I... I wanted to say, 'thank you'." The girl said.

"F-for what?" Twyla asked, but she already knew.

The girl stepped up to the bed. She didn't know what to do with her hands, so she held them together. Her eyes were downcast, as if she thought looking at Twyla would turn her to stone.

"I... I'm sorry about Chet and Nate. I thought—I didn't think they'd—" The girl wiped away a tear. "It's my fault."

"No." Twyla reached out and took the girl by the hand. "No. It's not. It isn't your fault."

The girl fell into sobs. Her face turned scarlet with shame, fear, and self-loathing. Twyla wished she could blot away those negative emotions. She wished she could cleanse the girl of all the trauma that Hank had given her.

Instead, Twyla just recalled the satisfying *crunch* of Hank's head beneath the weight of the passenger door. She had thought that killing her boyfriend would hurt her heart, even though he'd been no better than roadkill before his death. But her conscience was clear. Twyla had done what was right, and she refused to feel bad for it.

"It's not your fault." Twyla pulled the girl into an embrace. Her stomach cramped, which only made Twyla grip the girl tighter. "It's not your fault." She said into the girl's ear.

"It's not your fault..."

TOXIC

Afterword

Some of my first experiences in horror where in short form. I read Stephen King's *Night Shift* before checking out any of his longer narratives. I bought *Ellery Queen* magazines from a local flea-market, as well as flaky, old *EC* horror comics. Short horror has always been a part of my DNA as a reader and a writer. So, starting a collection is like returning home. It's a nostalgic experience, even when the stories are totally new to me.

One of my favorite parts of any collection is the notes authors leave behind, which discuss the inspiration for each tale. So, I'm not going to waste your time with a lot of words. I'm going to get right to it. Here are the notes on the conceptions of all nine stories in *Toxic*.

Spoilers! Don't read these notes until after you've finished the stories, ya goof!

An Occasional Portal
I figured that it would be a good idea to start the collection off with something less extreme. Consider this an appetizer. It's still bloody, but it feels less like *Creepshow* and more like *The Twilight Zone*. This was originally written for a website run by the folks that published my first two books. As far as I've seen... that website is now deleted. The story was then included in my now out of print collection *Your God Can't Save You*.

INNARDS-FUCK and *Anti-VaXXX* were also part of that collection, as was S*ardines (In the Dark)*, which I expanded enough to publish on its own. I definitely want to bring the rest of the stories from that collection back to print, so don't buy the overpriced version of it on eBay. Just be patient. Anyways... A*n Occasional Portal* is very much a more traditional and old-fashioned tale, and I'm pretty proud of it. My mother is a huge fan of vampires, so this is one I hope she'll get the courage to check out someday.

INNARDS-FUCK...

This is based on a true story. Kind of. Back when I was in high-school, I sat behind a weird kid in a social studies class. He oftentimes watched crazy shit on his phone. One day, I looked over his shoulder and saw he was watching "stump-fucking" anal porn. I never saw any snuff on his phone, thank God, but I'm sure he wouldn't look away if he encountered it.

What Are You Going to Do with Me? ...

I love watching old comedy films, but with that comes certain scenes that... haven't aged well. One of those moments is definitely in John Landis's *Animal House*. There's a part where John Belushi peeps on a group of undressing girls, and he breaks the forth wall to mug at the camera. Hey, as a woman... that's not funny. It's creepy. But fuck it... don't tell anyone I said this but... it's also kind of funny because it's John Belushi, and he could make

TOXIC

a laugh out of *anything*! Am I a bad woman for saying that? Eh. Probably. Anyways, I decided to write a story about frat-boy voyeurs without the humorous tone *Animal House* applied to the scene. I did not intend for this story to get as extreme as it did, but sometimes stories push boundaries whether you want them to or not. I actually struggled sleeping after writing this one. It just hurt my heart so much. Maybe it will have the same effect on you, and maybe it won't. Either way, I think it might be one of my darkest shorts. Unlike most of these, there's no punchline.

Toxic...
I watch a lot of apocalyptic movies, just as I watch a lot of old-school comedies. Sometimes, when shit gets really rough in those movies, I wonder why the lead characters don't just give up and walk directly into the mouth of annihilation. This story is basically a "what if" scenario. What if we followed the account of a side character instead of the survivor of an apocalyptic narrative? Yes. It's depressing. But I'd rather more kaiju movies showed the reality of what people would do when monsters rise from the ocean and destroy our cities.

The Cum House...
The name of this story was a joke with my roommate... and I honestly didn't think I'd do anything with the title. Of course, my go-to target is redneck horror, so combining that with an inside

joke was an almost natural action. This is also a great example of what I call a "punchline" story. I hope it made you laugh. Sometimes, I don't want to scare people, or make them feel depressed. I want to make them laugh. And that's exactly what *The Cum House* was built for. Laughin'. And cummin'. But not shittin'. Or pissin'.

Side note, and I acknowledge I'm bragging here but... Edward Lee told me he needed a bath after reading this story. Probably the proudest moment of my career.

Anti-VaXXX...

This is another punchline story. It's definitely satire too. As a trans woman, I grew up being told that the sexual acts I was attracted to were "sick". So... here's an example of *actual* "sick sex". I'd like to expand this idea into a full-length novel someday. There's a lot of room to wiggle around in with this concept.

Wee-Gee...

If you know me, you know I like the undead. But I don't like to write zombies or ghosts that follow strict rules. My sensibilities fall more in line with Lucio Fulci and Andrea Bianchi when it comes to the shambling dead. So W*ee-Gee* was written with the same mindset I employed for *Magick* and *Jump Scare*. It's more about the nightmarish visuals than it is about logic. And anyways, who cares about logic when one is reading or watching

TOXIC

horror? Horror doesn't—and shouldn't—make sense.

Sally...
This is one of the first horror stories I ever wrote. I think I read it aloud in eighth grade. Of course, the version of the story you just read isn't the exact story copy-and-pasted from my old computer to this one. In fact, the original version of *Sally* is long lost. I think I actually wrote it on a school computer, printed it, and then eventually threw that manuscript out while I was cleaning my room. I hadn't thought of this tale until recently, and then it wouldn't leave my brain. Like one of the mosquitos that tormented Pat, it latched on and irritated me until I had no choice but to scratch. So, I reconstructed it from memory. I hope it would make the young, aspirational writer I was in middle-school proud. And no, it's not at all extreme... but I'm happy as hell with it.

Cruising for Creeps...
1950's nostalgia is an odd thing. I felt it myself when I read Stephen King's *The Body* and watched the film adaptation. But Stephen King's book was more honest about the backside of that era than most people give him credit for. It's not just about the friendships youths form, it's about how memories are tainted by hardships, and how tragedy can spoil idealism. *Cruising For Creeps* aims for nothing quite as lofty, but I love the idea of taking something idyllic... and twisting it up.

TOXIC

There's a lot of this story that signifies nostalgia and good times but then it's about abusive men, vigilante justice, and trauma. *Cruising For Creeps* is one I'd categorize more as a crime story than a horror story, but it's extreme regardless. Even though there's a slow build to it. This is also one of the rare times I cracked a tear during the process of writing a story. Hearing "it's not your fault" will do that to me. Sometimes, I write just to tell myself that being abused was not my fault and—whew. Sorry, we got a little heavy there. Anyways, *Cruising For Creeps* is my favorite out of the nine stories featured in this collection. Which is why I decided to save it for last.

Thank you, dear reader, for coming along this dark path with me.

If you want to keep up with me and my next projects, follow me on Twitter and Facebook—under the name Judith Sonnet. Social media has been an absolute hellscape of bad vibes lately, so come on over and bring your positivity with ya!

I tend to just post updates on upcoming books or share the vintage paperbacks I spend too much money on at flea markets. It's a hoot and a half!

I'm also on Letterboxd, where you can read my uncensored thoughts on movies. Again, that's just under my name.

Thank you, again, to Duncan Ralston. Thank you for always being willing to talk with me, joke with me, and listen to my ideas. Your books are incredible, but your kindness and generosity are just as astounding. Writers, if you need a good pal, Duncan's your guy! I'm proud to be a *"woomie"*.

Thank you to Don Taylor for all the hype. It always cheers me up to hear you're excitement for the next book!

Thank you to A. A. Medina, for designing this spectacular cover!

Thank you to Anna R. Reid. Girls need to stand up for each other, and I've always felt supported by you in the short time we've known each other!

Thank you to Sean Duregger, for treating me seriously.

Thank you Carrie White Shields, KillerBunny Usagi, Pam Rutherford Cunningham, Corrina Morse, Bayou Muddah Turner-Jones, Liza Zaruba, Robyn Lemley, and Cynthia Dienes. I'm so happy to have such wonderful readers!

Thank you to Wrath James White, for being on my side.

Thank you to Jon Athan, for all the scares!

A huge round of thanks to Mr. Edward Lee. Hearing you say that one of my stories grossed you out literally made me weep with joy. You're an absolute legend, and a joy to talk to! Can't wait for *Amityville Bukkake*!

And thank you to Christina Marie! You already know why, you wonderful human you!

With love,
From Utah
Judith Sonnet

TOXIC

TOXIC

Cover and wrap design by:

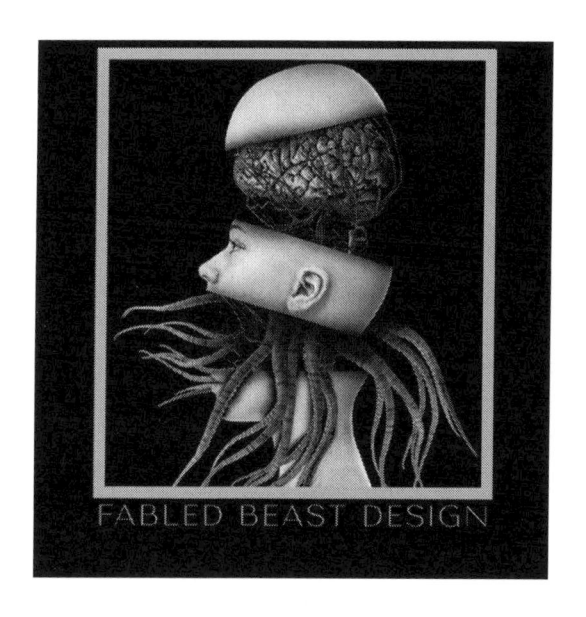

FABLED BEAST DESIGN

Made in the USA
Middletown, DE
17 February 2024